THE GAME OF LIFE...

The Game of Life...

The Final Clue

Kristin Corson-Ricci

Published by Game Changer Publishing

Paperback ISBN: 978-1-969372-29-2

Hardcover ISBN: 978-1-969372-30-8

Digital ISBN: 978-1-969372-31-5

www.GameChangerPublishing.com

For my three kids, Emily, Sophia, and Nick

...whose laughter is my favorite sound,
who continue to inspire me each and every day and
who taught me that with the right perspective,
even the quietest moments reveal how deeply
blessed we are—this is for you.

Also for my biggest cheerleader, my mom, as well
as my fiancé, Steve, and my close friends.
Your loving encouragement made this book possible.

Thank you for buying and reading my book!
Scan the QR code to connect:

THE GAME OF LIFE...

THE FINAL CLUE

KRISTIN CORSON-RICCI

CONTENTS

PROLOGUE
KRISTY

November 27, 2024

You can tell a lot about a home by how it smells.

This house smells like a delicious mixture of Frasier Fir candles and Stove Top stuffing.

My mother loves to cook, so cook she does. In quantities to feed what seems like most of New Jersey. And if you know anything about New Jersey, it may be small in size, but man, it is populated.

Today is my favorite day. Thanksgiving Eve. You would know this just by stepping into our home. The clanging of pots, the dropping of stainless-steel spoons, and the aroma of what will be the makings of a perfect Thanksgiving dinner. My mom taught me at a young age to make everything you can the night before.

Everything. Then, when family and friends arrive, they smell the reheated homemade goodness, and she can socialize. "Never get stuck in the kitchen while everyone else gets to have fun," she would say. She has gone so far as to label each Tupperware in the fridge with a Post-it, detailing the exact reheating instructions so that she doesn't even have to do the final prep. Brilliant!

Perfect Family. Perfect Thanksgiving Eve. Perfect-smelling house.

"When will Tom be back with the potato bread? How am I supposed to make his favorite stuffing without my main ingredient?" she yells, head in the pantry.

"Mom, he's been gone like ten minutes. Relax!"

"No, actually, he's been gone for fifty minutes. You've been scrolling on your phone for the better part of an hour."

At that exact moment, the doorbell rings, followed by intense banging on the door.

"Can I help you?" Mom says with disdain as she answers the door. She doesn't like to leave the stove unattended.

"Are you Mrs. Shore?" a handsome police officer questions at the door.

"Yes, my name is Helen, but I assure you I have a permit to park in the street. If you'll just give me a second, I can grab it for you," Mom says as she turns her back to the officer to retrieve her parking permit.

"No ma'am, that's not why I'm here," the officer explains, stopping Mom in her tracks. "It's your husband, Thomas. He was in an accident. And I'm so sorry, but he did not survive."

CHAPTER 1

KRISTY

Two Weeks Earlier

Today started like every single day of these past few months. Cozette, although three, is acting in true terrible twos fashion, screaming bloody murder from her bedroom. Waking up the entire apartment complex before the sun even rises in her attempt to display her desperate desire, of all things, to get a dog.

Hilarious. To just be in the mind of a three-year-old for one minute would be so refreshing. I can't remember a time when my most stressful concern was longing for a pet. I want to yell back at her, "You have no idea! Life, my dear, is going to get so very hard! Enjoy your carefree life of being three with zero problems. And for the love of God, STOP SCREAMING!" But instead, I go into her room as quickly as possible and reply with, "Maybe, sweetie." It's just so much easier than trying to reason with a toddler.

I will say, this kid sure is cute, even when she's having one of her tantrums. Her white-blonde hair hangs in uneven pigtails, and her cheeks, flushed from all the screaming, are still absolutely adorable.

A dog might just be the worst decision I could ever make at this point in my life. What, with my six-hundred-square-foot, walk-up, fifth-floor apartment and my job requiring me to be out of the house for much of the day? I'm pretty sure *any* dog could find a home more fitting to live in. I'm pretty sure any *human* could find a home more fitting to live in. But not me.

Being the oldest of three kids, I have taken on the role of responsible daughter. And although I can be relied on almost all the time, I have been known to carve out my own path on more than one occasion.

I was named after Kristy McNichol, who apparently had the best hair on television in the '70s. Much to my mother's chagrin, my hair decided not to follow suit. It, too, decided to carve its own path. Unlike my sister's and Mom's perfectly straight blond locks, mine fall more into the category of unruly, dirty-blond, erratic-curl variety, which my dad says adds to my spunky personality. I am in awe of his rose-colored glasses.

But sadly, I have been dealt a less-than-stellar hand. If not for my parents keeping my head on straight for the past three years, I really don't know where I'd be. I'm guessing on a street corner, somewhere. Making ten times what I make now.

Wait? Maybe my parents are doing me a disservice?

Anyway, waiting tables pays the rent. But not much more than that. My culinary school degree has taken a much longer sabbatical than I would've liked. But with mouths to feed, continuing school seemed a bit selfish and impractical at the time.

But I'm an optimist and keep telling myself that it could be so much worse.

It could be, right? Right.

So we spend most of our dog-free life waiting for our luck to turn a corner. Well, I do. Cozette just spends most of her dog-free life screaming for her life to not be dog-free.

Our morning consists of making breakfast, packing lunches, cleaning up my disastrous kitchen, and throwing clothes on Cozette to get her to preschool. Some days I get to work, and the morning seems like a blur of eggs and hair ribbons.

But this morning is different. This is Wednesday morning. The most glorious day of my week. Every single week. I spend it daydreaming about Leo. Daydreaming about our soon-to-be fabulous night together.

Having Dad pick up Cozette from preschool every Wednesday so I can have some semblance of a social life has been the best gift I've ever been given. And keeping her overnight for their fun sleepover parties has been a godsend. I adore my daughter. Really, I do. But my god, do my ears need a break occasionally.

I find myself fantasizing about Wednesday nights—on Thursdays.

Leo and I have only been dating for two years, but they have, without a doubt, been the best two years of my life. I have yet to find a single flaw in that man. And it's not for a lack of trying. Being the unstable half of the relationship can be exhausting. I should know. I've been practicing that role for two years now. And man, I'm getting really good at it.

So tonight, I get to see him and spend the night with him, playing house, until reality punches me in the face Thursday afternoon at preschool pick-up.

Tonight will be different, though. Most Wednesdays, we go out to dinner, like weekly little celebrations of making it through another week. But tonight, I'm cooking. It's something I love doing, and he loves being on the receiving end. Of course, it's not his *favorite* thing he likes receiving from me, but it's a close second.

Cooking for a three-year-old's palate can be underwhelming. But with Leo, I indulge my passion for cooking by going to the farmers market for the freshest herbs and to the butcher for the best cuts of meat. It is extremely satisfying to put so much care and thought into his meals. I know he truly appreciates it from the compliments he gives between each bite.

Tonight, I am trying my hand at Beef Wellington. A daunting task, sure, but I'm up for it. And maybe if the night goes as perfectly as I'm thinking it will, he will be on bended knee shortly after dinner. Not that my Wellington will be *that* delicious—I mean, I'm hoping it will be, and I'm expecting it to be, but I am not so naive as to think that one mere dish will make him propose.

But two years is two years, so I'm hopeful.

CHAPTER 2

No ring.

But it's fine. I keep telling myself, it's totally fine.

He loves me. Of that, I'm completely confident. But is he super conservative and practical? Yeah.

Who cares that it hasn't happened? I *know* it wasn't because of my Beef Wellington. That shit was perfect. So much so that I've decided that when I open my dream restaurant, it will be my specialty. One day.

In the meantime, I found a way to lower the volume of our mornings in the apartment.

Today, when the blood-curdling screams began, I went into Cozette's room with what I think may be the perfect gift.

A Real Dog.

These things are all the rage and not easy to find—anywhere. Ever since the Christmas commercials began three months ago in August, they've been flying off the shelves. It's apparently this year's hottest toy. Gone are the days of Cabbage Patch Kids and Tickle Me Elmos. Now, if you're willing to break the bank, you can own the closest thing to an actual dog that you will ever see. Well, the closest thing Cozette will ever see, anyway.

Wow. Why the heck didn't I think of this sooner? Taking this Real Dog, with its collar in a beautiful shade of electric cerulean, out of her Christmas gift pile early was genius. Thank God Dad suggested it. I'm a traditionalist and thought the idea was absurd. Give her a gift for screaming? And take it out of my hard-earned-cash Christmas gift pile? Yes. That's exactly what I did. And boy, I wish Dad had suggested I do this months ago.

Tears stopped. On a dime. "The doggie I wanted!" Followed by suffocating squeezes from Cozette.

Wait, the whole time, *this* is what she wanted? Not an actual dog. But the commercially driven, impossible-to-find stuffed animal that barks? Maybe I should be paying closer attention to what she watches on TV. I think my quality of life has just improved tenfold. As did that of my neighbors. I feel the need to announce to the fifth floor, "Ladies and gentlemen, set your alarms for tomorrow! For you will no longer be waking up to the joyous sounds of a screaming toddler."

But I think better of it and instead just make her eggs.

Okay, so I'm not sure my dad understands the severity of the life-changing event that happened earlier in the week when I gifted the Real Dog to Cozette. She slept past 5:30. Awoke happy as could be for maybe the first time ever, holding Fudge as tightly as she could. Fudge. She went with "Fudge." Seriously? A completely white, fluffy dog, "Fudge"? Not, maybe, "Snowball" or "Fluffy"? Or even the fan favorite, "Max"?

But **okay**, you want to name him "Fudge." Not my toy, not my obsession, not my apparent lifeline, as she will not leave home without him.

But what she *has* been doing is staying quietly in her room until 6:45. Every single morning since Fudge. Which means I am sleeping restfully until 6:30.

Beauty sleep is so underrated. My skin looks better, my eyes aren't puffy with black bags, and my mood is much less curmudgeonly.

Just wait until Leo sees the new-and-improved Kristy Shore!

CHAPTER 3

The phone call. That annual "Let's split up the Thanksgiving dinner list" phone call.

My younger brother, without hesitation or the slightest bit of guilt, inevitably snags rolls and olives. While my younger sister and I hem and haw over how many varieties of potatoes we really need. And does anyone even eat the green bean casserole? I've been told the answers are "three" and "yes." Then the dividing begins. Mom will be hosting, as she does every year, so she gets the biggies—turkey and ham. My sister and I will divvy up everything else. My list is sure to be double-sided.

If our family is known for just one thing, it's definitely lack-of-food-phobia.

Dad's annual contribution to each and every holiday is scratch-off lottery tickets. It wouldn't be a Shore family gathering without a few losers, a few "one card free" prizes, and one big winner of $25. Then, like clockwork, we reminisce over the year a cousin brought a soon-to-be ex-boyfriend, and he won $500. Of course he did. Did I mention my apartment is six hundred square feet, and buying the Real Dog broke the bank?

Dad loves his scratch-off contribution. You'll find him standing in the corner, chest puffed with confidence, showing just the slightest hint of the "dad bod" he's destined to acquire, much to the dismay of his buddies, who encountered theirs years ago. Along with their white hair, Dad still clings to the few strands of pepper he has left. He stands smiling as the family scratches away, using, of course, the dime he taped to the back of the ticket. It feels like a scene out of a Hallmark movie, the kind that looks almost too perfect to be real.

The only thing more predictable than Dad's love of distributing scratch-offs is his love of his weekly lottery pool at work. Every week since the beginning of time, he has gone to work on Monday mornings with a crisp five-dollar bill in his pocket for the possibility of millions.

Dad and his coworkers have yet to win those millions. But the dreaming of what he'll do with said millions is half the fun. At least that's what he says. I firmly believe the actual beach house that we would have from the winnings would be more than half the fun.

Unfortunately, growing up, the office lottery pool has given us nothing except two steak dinners.

But the pride on his face as he walked in the back door with steaks from his tiny, split fifteen-ways jackpot (twice) was all I needed to see to encourage him to continue the weekly five-dollar donation.

Selfishly, I'd love for him to hit the Mega Millions, which has recently become Mega Billions, just as much as he would. Dad has always had lofty dreams of exotic purchases with his winnings. But lately he has been stuck on four very specific things. And these things are discussed ad nauseam. It's unhealthy how often Dad tries to squeeze lottery talk into every conversation, which concerns me, as I really don't think he has a single other hobby.

His specific things are very selfless, as that is most definitely my dad's best characteristic. My mother will be gifted with any beach house she would like on any beach in the world.

But as my mom is not nearly as exotic as Dad, she will, one hundred percent, pick Cape May, New Jersey. She says there is no place she'd rather be: "The Jersey beaches have everything I could ever want in a vacation home, and it's only a short drive away!" She finds herself defending her choice in every conversation.

Yeah, I guess. If you have something against palm trees and fancy accents, the Jersey Shore is where you want to be.

My brother, Joe, will be given the gift of a baby. Well, not *exactly* a baby, but the money for IVF, which will all but ensure a growing family and more grandkids. He and his lovely wife, Leah, have been trying for years with no luck.

I, on the other hand, was certainly *not* trying to conceive, but my long-term boyfriend's sperm had a different plan. And long-term or not, if you don't want to be a dad, you don't want to be a dad. Hence, my single motherhood title.

I have never played the victim in this situation, because I am certainly not a victim. But I was okay with a surprise baby, and he was not. I can't fault him for being honest, although I *can* fault him for never meeting his adorable, spunky, dog-loving spawn. Again, not a victim, I just like to vent every now and again. I owe him a thank you, quite frankly. Coparenting can be so messy. After all, you're not parenting together because you don't agree on things. What makes raising a child in two different houses, while still *not* agreeing, any easier?

Dad has promised my sister a substantial down payment on an "actual adult house," as he calls it.

My little sis, Sandra, has hit the "sweet spot" of her life. She's old enough to have college behind her and young enough to still go out every single night of the week. She doesn't have to live at home with our parents and their parental rules, and her bills are still reasonably manageable.

Sandra is dating, but not seriously enough to meet the family. And like my brother, she has no kids.

She lives in a swanky part of Philadelphia, where all the twenty-some-things look like pharmaceutical sales reps. She is in no hurry to leave this wonderful lifestyle, but firmly believes that when she is, Dad will have won big, and therefore she'll just strut into her new home, debt-free.

As for my lotto-winning portion? My very own restaurant and a great set of knives; every good chef needs a great set of knives, above all else, usually the first major purchase from every chef's first paycheck.

Fortunately, my goals have changed quite a bit since I was a child.

Because if my dad *had* won the lottery when I was five to eight years of age, I'd be the proud owner of a traveling circus. Yes, a circus. That's all I ever wanted to do with my life. My dream was to be a clown in the circus —it seemed so glamorous.

How could there be any better job than making people laugh as a clown? Who doesn't love clowns? Come to find out, about 99.9 percent of the population does *not* love clowns. Live and learn. But I will say, one of the saddest days of my childhood was the day I found out The Clown College in Sarasota had closed.

A restaurant is a much better investment, and I'm sure my dad agrees.

Although he would never announce this to the family, I know he secretly had a lotto wish number five.

For himself, I know he would splurge on a proper wedding that he says my mom deserves. He talked once about renewing their vows at a fancy country club, and I'm guessing the cost is the reason he hasn't acted on it.

I can hear Dad in the background, laughing as Mom and I are on the phone discussing the color choice of napkins for Thanksgiving. Dad is always laughing.

I have never met a person who wakes up with a smile and goes to bed with a smile, other than my dad. No problem is too much for that man to handle. There has never been a situation where he could not find the lemonade beyond the lemons. Dad has, on more than one occasion, quoted Bill Vaughn, who famously said, "A real patriot is the fellow who gets a parking ticket and rejoices that the system works." I never really understood that quote until recently. If that doesn't speak to his optimism, I don't know what does. He and I have always shared such a grand love of life. I mean, yes, everyone loves life. But I mean, he *really* loves life... He wakes up every morning thanking a higher being for all we are blessed with, goes outside every morning smiling at his first breath of fresh morning air, and most importantly, goes to bed each night thanking his lucky stars for the health of our family and friends.

Tonight, though, his laughter comes from jokes told by his coworker Marty. Marty, who's at least six inches shorter than my dad and much rounder, visits often; some would say too often. There are times I feel like he comes to see my mom as much as, if not more than, my dad. My dad would call him a close friend. My biggest objection to Marty is his scent. Does *anything* smell worse than Fahrenheit cologne for men?

Doesn't seem to bother anyone but me, which is fine; he is practically part of the family. After his wife passed away from cancer years ago, he has attended most of our family events, from holiday dinners to movie nights, and even joined us on a few family vacations.

As far as Cozette knows, he is and always has been Uncle Marty.

CHAPTER 4

November 27, 2024

"No, ma'am. That's not why I'm here. It's your husband, Tom. He was in an accident. And I'm so sorry; he did not survive."

Words that don't seem quite real as they are being said aloud.

Words that sound like they are in a foreign language.

Like, I know the officer is talking, but I'm certain he's got it all wrong.

He has the wrong house. He has the wrong family. He has the wrong Mrs. Shore.

CHAPTER 5

MARTY

"Hello, Helen! How are you?"

I answer my phone, yet again, loving the technology of caller ID.

Crazy to think that for most of my sixty-plus years of life, I answered my landline phone without knowing who was on the other end.

"Marty." A shaky and almost unrecognizable voice crackles through the line. After a heavy pause, Helen continues to speak. Her words come in jagged bursts, as if forced through clenched teeth.

"I know you just left here a few hours ago, but I—I need to tell you something."

A sharp inhale, then a ragged exhale. There's faint movement like she's pacing, clutching the phone like a lifeline.

Helen's voice trembles. "I have horrific news." Another pause. A muffled sound, like she's pressing a hand over her mouth, holding back a sob. "It's Tom." A choked swallow. "He never came home from going to the store."

Silence stretches between them, thick and unbearable. When she finally wills herself to speak again, her voice is not her own, hoarse and barely a whisper, as if saying the words out loud makes them more real.

"He was in a terrible car accident... and he didn't make it, Marty," she states as if gasping for air. "Marty, Tom died!"

There is a rustling sound—she's collapsing into a chair, pressing a hand to her chest, trying to breathe through the weight of it.

Silence.

I'd be lying if I said I wasn't in shock. The kind of shock where you get very confused. Questioning who you're talking to on the phone and what they've just said. Repeating "Tom died!" over and over in your head. That kind of shock.

"Marty? Are you there?"

"Umm, yeah, I'm here. Shit, Helen. I'm so sorry; I don't even know what to say. He died? But I just saw him?"

"Yes. This is a nightmare. I called Joe and Sandra, and they were inconsolable on the phone. Kristy went to pick them up and bring them here. I don't want them driving right now," Helen says, seemingly just as shocked as I feel.

"Okay, wow. I'm going to need a minute to process this." I, too, am now pacing aimlessly throughout my rather small kitchen. Rubbing my forehead as if it will provide some clarity. "What can I do? How can I help you?"

"Nothing at the moment. But I will be calling on you soon for help, I'm sure. The kids are pulling in the driveway, so I'm going to go. Bye, Marty."

"OK, please call me tonight or tomorrow, or whenever you have a minute."

I just stare into space as she ends the call.

My best friend just died. Gone.

Coworker, friend, brother, for all intents and purposes.

Life without him will never be the same.

CHAPTER 6

KRISTY

To say we are completely devastated is the understatement of the century.

The week goes by as a blur of family visits and casseroles. Why does everyone, I mean everyone, bring a casserole when a loved one passes? No one feels much like eating. And when they do, I assure you, they aren't rushing to the fridge for the tuna casserole Mary, the neighbor five doors down, made in a pinch. I suppose it's nice, but why not just give the family a bunch of DoorDash gift cards? That way, when I want a salad and my brother, Joe, wants a burrito, everyone is happy. My mom seems to appreciate the revolving door of casseroles, and I guess that's all that matters.

Funerals are exhausting. The planning, the logistics, the sadness of the ultimate finality of it all. It can be too much. Joe, Sandra, and I try to be the best support system for Mom while attempting to keep it together ourselves. When it is over, the four of us collapse on Mom's sofa.

Our heads are spinning. We stay up half the night, telling the best Dad stories we have. All so different, depending on who is telling it. So many friends and family came to offer their condolences, which makes me smile.

It's nice to see how many people's lives Dad touched. It brings comfort to Mom to see so many friendly faces.

I just can't help thinking about what a zemblanity it was. Dad went out for potato bread and his beloved lottery tickets and never came home.

When Officer O'Mally said Dad was likely avoiding an animal in the road and therefore swerved into the concrete median, dying instantly, I just about lost it. I had to immediately sit or run the risk of passing out and vomiting simultaneously. Although I am relieved to hear he likely did not suffer, it pains me to think this stupid animal in the road probably just scampered off without a clue.

Knowing our beloved father died is one thing; picturing his final seconds is something else completely.

I guess this is my life now. Family of four. One parent. Solemn holidays. Lots of reminiscing.

I don't think anyone ever prepares for the time when they will lose their favorite person in the whole world. Well, at least I didn't. And poor Cozette keeps asking for Pop. I've tried to explain in so many words that Pop is not coming back. But the questions keep coming, all day, every day. And with every question, I feel like I'm losing him again and again.

CHAPTER 7

My mom has decided it's time to start clearing away Dad's bathroom things and maybe take a stab at his home office. Apparently, seeing his toothbrush first thing every morning is crazy hard for her.

I can't even imagine.

I am her go-to with projects like this. She knows I am sentimental and will listen to all her stories about each item we donate or throw away. But she also knows I'm practical and will not keep things like his used razor just because.

Projects like this are exactly what I need. They give me another reason to get up in the morning and change out of my pajamas. And a reason not to drop off Cozette at school and footslog back to bed.

"Honey, thank you for your help. I just can't bear to throw anything away. But I also can't bear to have these reminders all over the house, especially in the bathroom. It seems these intimate items are the hardest to part with," Mom says, as her eyes fill with tears.

"It's no problem, Mom. Let's just look at it like we are spring cleaning. And we're only going to keep what you use on a consistent basis. We'll clean the whole bathroom, not just Dad's things."

She agrees, begrudgingly.

We have cleared the bathroom. It only took a little over an hour (due to the stories about why he would only use Camay soap and how hard it was to find when it was discontinued, etc.), although I could have done it solo in about ten minutes. This is good therapy for her. She needs this.

What she *doesn't* need is shredding all his cleared checks, bank books, and statements. I plan to conquer the office on my own, or it'll take forever to clean out. Maybe I'll break the news to her to gather what she wants to keep tonight so I can start working on it tomorrow. After all, Cozette's babysitter is not doing volunteer work. And right now, this is not money well spent.

~

A short ten hours later, I am back at Mom's to get started.

I walk into the house and take off my shoes, planning to be here for a while. The carpeted steps show their age, as the middle of each stair is worn down and not nearly as plush as its risers.

I go into the office, embracing my dad's aftershave scent.

Dad's office, my old bedroom, is my favorite room in the whole house. Whenever visiting in the past, I would always find an excuse to come up here and just take a look around. The adolescent memories it holds are priceless. That, combined with Dad's undeniable scent, makes it even more homey.

I sit crisscross on the floor to begin my sorting and tossing.

Holy smokes! So. Many. Paper. Documents.

So many trees found their demise, just based on this first of four filing cabinets.

Thank God I decided to do this alone. It may take *me* forever just to shred all this paperwork, even without Mom's stories. I decide to start with the back of the first filing cabinet and make my way closer to the present day.

I believe he has saved every single bank statement and bill invoice dating back to 1972. Some of these banks and companies are no longer even in business.

The paper shredder fills up eight times before lunch, as I have been on autopilot reading, shredding, reading, and shredding. My eyes are crossing, and I need a quick break.

I love my coworkers for many reasons, but especially the understanding and flexibility they've shown me these past weeks. They let me keep a shift here and there, but for the most part, they have given me the time to grieve and save Mom from things like cleaning out the office, so she does not have to.

My brother and sister are not the most reliable in times like these. Ignorance is bliss, I suppose. Sandra and Joe, although certainly struck with grief, have a unique way of showing it. They have been in their own little worlds, offering Mom very little help.

Sandra is an elementary school teacher and apparently the busiest person on the face of the earth. Challenging, maybe. Tiring? I'm sure. But nights and weekends? *Where ya at now, sis?* And Joe? Just plain clueless. His wife is very type A and a take-charge kind of girl. And so, she does. Unless she tells him to come help Mom, he'll stay right where he is, waiting for his next instruction.

Working at this all morning, I am making some serious headway, and I'm already on cabinet number three when it's time to work my lunch shift.

Walking into Chickie's and Pete's, I notice the crowd of guests gathered around the hostess stand. A fellow waitress, Colleen, walks by me, rolling her eyes in despair. "Throw on your apron; Table 5 is waiting for you. They haven't even been served water yet," she unhappily reports.

"This is great, because my decline in shifts has left me with a decline in my checking account. I'll take all the tables I can get today!" I respond cheerily. It is obvious who is just reporting to work and who has been here doing the work of two until right now.

My shift kept me so busy that I didn't even have time to eat, which would have gone unnoticed by me if Colleen hadn't asked me a dozen times if I needed a break to grab a bite. My appetite has been nonexistent since my dad passed. My meals lately are eaten out of necessity, not cravings.

The good thing about being nonstop at work is that it helps take my mind off losing my dad.

When my shift is over and it's time to pick up Cozette, I am downright spent. I just want to see her, get some hugs, and go home to throw on slippers.

She's been in quite a funk for a few weeks, although we did have a great run of good moods. I was beginning to think we had turned a corner, and the toddler tantrums were on their way out. Wishful thinking. Hearing the screams when walking into aftercare just made me want to turn around, hoping none of the teachers saw me.

But to my chagrin, every single staff member is staring right at me when they hear the door.

Desperation in their faces. The oldest of the women, and I assume the one in charge of aftercare, does not hesitate to approach me. "Hello, Ms. Shore. We've had quite a day. And by quite a day, I mean screaming for the past six hours. Can I please ask that you only bring Cozette *with* her white dog? She is incredibly hard to console without it."

"Right. So, about that, my dad just passed; we've all been in quite a tizzy. Believe it or not, we haven't been able to find it. And as you may know, they aren't cheap! I'm hopeful it will turn up, so I don't have to save up for another!" I reply cheerfully. With each word that comes out of my mouth, she seems to get angrier and angrier. This woman means business. "OK, I'm on it! Number one priority: find Fudge!"

Still nothing, not a single movement from this woman, who is clearly over me and most definitely over Cozette.

"Hear that, Cozette? We need to find that doggie so I can bring you back!" Still nothing.

CHAPTER 8

MARTY

It's hard to find the right thing to say and the right thing to do in times like these. I have reached out to Helen a half dozen times, asking what she needs from me, and I have yet to hear back from her. I know this first-hand, from when my wife passed away. I never asked for any help or guidance during that trying time, but neighbors came through for me anyway, bringing a meal, making sure I had the groceries I needed, or simply offering a shoulder to cry on. Sometimes people must be told what they need. So that's what I'm going to do.

I make a huge lasagna, sure to last a few nights, even if Helen invites me over to stay for dinner. After all, why wouldn't I stay? As much as I enjoy cooking for Helen, if I'm just feeding myself, it's TV dinners every night. I would love some of this lasagna. And instead of making myself a smaller portion, I'm optimistic that she will extend an invitation. After all, her kids are back at work, so she'll probably be eating alone otherwise.

The lasagna and bagged salad are wrapped up and ready to deliver. My excuse to go over, of course, is to bring Helen dinner. But my goal is to stay and help her clean out some things and tick them off her to-do list.

As I drive over to Helen's, I can't stop thinking about the last heart-to-heart that Tom and I had at work. He opened up to me as we sat in the break room, eating our brown-bagged lunches.

"Marty, you know how I've been complaining about Helen being so absent-minded lately? Forgetting where she's left *everything*, and not even remembering my birthday?" This comes out of nowhere. Like it's been festering in his mind and needs to free itself. He looks both concerned and saddened at the same time as he talks about Helen. His shoulders slump as if it were exhausting him to relive it.

"You have a right to be frustrated about the birthday thing, but you've had like one hundred together, so maybe she's just tired of celebrating you." I tried unsuccessfully to make light of the situation.

"I wish that were the case. But sadly, it's more than that," Tom says in a more serious tone than I have ever heard from him.

"I took her to a neurologist, and he diagnosed her with early-onset dementia."

"Oh shit, Tom. That is horrible. I'm sorry. What do they say the symptoms are, and do they know if and when the symptoms will progress?"

Tom went on to describe the mental decline and confusion, along with irritability and hallucinations that are likely to present themselves. He already sees sporadic paranoia and sleep changes in Helen, and he fears the worst.

"It's like overnight she changed. Lately, she's had such poor judgment and intense mood swings that I fear telling her anything of importance. Or, God forbid, tell her anything personal or private; she has had no filter whatsoever. I heard her on the phone the other day, telling someone about my recent constipation issues. I mean, I can't get mad at her, but seriously?"

With that, Tom manages a slight grin.

~

Helen's decline may be slow, but she will need my guidance through most of this. It's what Tom would have wanted.

Whether she wants my help or not, she is going to get it.

I won't take no for an answer.

CHAPTER 9

KRISTY

Thank God, *finally, Wednesday*! I felt like this day would never come.

I dropped Cozette off with a different stuffed lovie, pretending I didn't understand the assignment. And I scoot out of there before they can ask where Fudge is.

Phew, crisis averted.

Now back to my daydreaming. I think a nice romantic dinner out is just what the doctor ordered. Talk about a celebration for making it through the week! I think I deserve a nice steak dinner tonight after the week I've had.

Just when I am about to text Leo to suggest this wonderful plan, my phone rings.

"Must be Mom," I mumble to myself.

She is just about the only person who uses the phone for what it was originally intended.

To my surprise, it's Leo! This could either be really good or really bad. In our two years together, I can count on one hand how many times I've heard his voice over the phone.

"Hi, honey. Bad news, I completely forgot about the Keller Williams dinner I have tonight. It'll be a late one. Sorry, I have to cancel our

Wednesday," he says, as I hear him typing on his computer in the background.

Not sure if words can express the disappointment I'm feeling. And apparently, my voice doesn't express it either, because within a second, he has to hang up. I feel as if I'm deflating, like an overfilled balloon with a slow but steady leak.

Selfishly, this is the worst news. But I suppose it is for the best. Maybe I'll bring Cozette to Mom's anyway so they can hang out while I try to finish the paperwork shredding.

Quite the opposite of the Wednesday night I had been daydreaming about.

My phone rings again! Twice in one day! Now the stats are 50/50. Maybe it will be Leo reconsidering our dinner plans!

No such luck, but I am feeling quite popular with all this phone ringing.

It's just Sandra.

"Hey!" I manage to hide my disappointment.

"Hey Kristy! I'm coming to Mom's the second I'm done with my lesson plans for next week. Work has been brutal, and to top it off, a kid bit me this morning! Thank goodness I've gotten a tetanus shot!" Sandra exclaims. "Oh, and thanks for picking up the slack with Mom. I haven't cooked her a single meal or even been much company to her these past few weeks.

"You know how December it is in elementary school. Every day, these kids become more and more wired. I wish I could just glue them to their desks. So yeah, thanks for all you are doing for her. Mom said you've started on Dad's office. That must be torture; he never threw anything away!"

Wow. She really does not come up for air. I could just put the phone down and walk away; there would be no way she'd know.

She's going to try to squeeze in helping Mom this evening, but I have such a groove going, she'd be better off just keeping Mom company and watching Cozette while I clean and declutter.

And if that one-sided conversation is any indication of how much coffee she's had today and how much she has to say, it'll be best if she stays downstairs.

We hang up, and I call Joe. I am hopeful that our conversation will be a bit more two-sided and that he'll be able to come over to keep Mom company while I'm busy upstairs.

"Hey Joe, it's Kristy. Just planned to leave you a message, because I *always* leave you messages. Why don't you ever pick up? I know you're there. Ugh! Anyway, Sandra and I are heading to Mom's to help her declutter and join her for dinner. Can you come? You don't need to bring anything, just yourself. I'm even bringing your favorite Cheesesteak Stromboli from Shamrock Deli. Okay, well, hope to see you at Mom's!"

Unfortunately, another one-sided conversation. At least this time I got a word in.

Even with the stromboli, no shot he comes.

CHAPTER 10

There's no turning back now. I vow to get this entire room cleaned out while I have some free sitters. That is the best motivation to get this project done! Plus, it'll keep my mind off missing Leo. I know he has an obligation to his work dinner, and I know that he would never cheat; I completely trust him with every fiber of my being. But my heart hurts, sometimes physically, when I go for long periods without seeing him. Knowing that we had a guaranteed Wednesday night together when Dad kept Cozette overnight was something I could always look forward to. Now, our kid-free time is more sporadic, making it also more cherished.

Cozette is happily playing with two of her favorite people, hoping that Uncle Joey will come to visit. I even brought an extra stromboli, on the off-chance Joe does show. And if he doesn't, at least Mom will have some variety from her casserole-stuffed fridge.

Back up the stairs I go, down the carpeted hallway, and into my dad's office. He never actually had to work from home, but he loved having the space for a desk and his perfectly sorted bills. My car wasn't fully backed out of the driveway before Dad had started transforming my childhood bedroom into his favorite room in the house. Feels like I'm intruding on his space while I go through his chronically sorted financial life.

The nice thing about sitting at his desk while I sort is that the entire room smells of him, a combination of Old Spice deodorant and Skin Bracer aftershave lotion.

Well, this is it. The final cabinet. I wasn't anticipating it to feel as bittersweet as it does. This has been a fairly pleasant, unexpected, intimate time I've gotten to share with my dad.

We never spoke of it aloud, but I know I was his favorite. We had a special connection and bond that he didn't seem to share with my siblings. Of course, he was close with my younger brother Joe and all his sports teams that Dad coached. And Sandra was his baby, so they have that spoiled-rotten kind of bond.

But mine was different. Possibly because I made him a dad. He and I didn't just connect on an intellectual level. We shared a sense of humor and love for life, and we found the good in everyone and everything. I used to be nothing but optimistic. These days, it takes more effort to have the same positive attitude. Time has started to make me cynical. I really need to work on that. If not for myself, then for my dad.

As I open this last filing cabinet, I notice it's not even halfway full. This will be cleaned out in no time, especially since the process is going by at a much quicker pace since I decided not to read each bank statement in detail.

When I started, I really didn't know the rabbit hole I was going down by studying each document. It's more difficult than I expected to shred Dad's belongings. Irrelevant and outdated, or not. I felt the need to read through every single paper before it meets its fate in many slivered pieces in the garbage.

I'm not ready for my office time to be over yet. This room is more special to me than to anyone else in the family. Even though this was my bedroom only starting in high school, those were pivotal years. I have just as many memories in this bedroom as I do in the bedroom that Sandra and I shared for the first twelve years of my life. Just sitting on the floor brings back floods of memories. Every stain on the cream-colored, wall-to-wall carpet has a story. The bright pink streak next to the desk is from when Alyson, my neighbor, and I were dancing to the

Backstreet Boys and accidentally knocked over my favorite bubble gum shade of nail polish. And, of course, the area of rug under my desk is worn from years and years of sitting at this desk doing homework or makeup, followed by years and years of Dad sitting here paying the bills or reading the newspaper. I absolutely love that we brought this desk with us when we moved, and I absolutely love that he kept my desk when cleaning out the rest of my bedroom furniture. If this piece of furniture could talk!

I hear giggles downstairs; I definitely have more time to dedicate to this clean-out. When I am finished with the cabinets, I sit at my dad's upgraded desk chair. I never would have thought of asking for a reclining swivel chair. My hard, uncomfortable wooden one seemed just fine. Plus, it had some of my favorite stickers plastered all over it, so I would've probably not let it go, even if my parents suggested a new one.

I lean back in his chair, and it takes me back to getting my own phone *in my room*! God, I remember what a big deal that was at the time. The epitome of privacy. Gone were the days of sitting on the hallway floor attached to a long phone cord, anchored on the kitchen wall. I could talk to boys now, in the privacy of my bedroom, with no one listening! Unless, of course, Joe decided to pick up the phone in the kitchen and eavesdrop.

"Joe! Hang up the phone!" I would scream at him. Pretending to hang up, I could still hear his breathing, so I would scream louder. "JOE!" until finally Mom or Dad intervened. That scenario happened more often than it didn't. To think that Cozette may never know the annoyance of a little brother in quite the same way.

I sit back upright, ready to head downstairs.

But first, let's see if my special scented erasers are still in my secret drawer. This is more commonly known as a keyboard tray now, but before I had a computer or keyboard of any kind, it was my secret drawer.

It sticks the same way it did decades ago.

Sadly, there are no erasers and no puffy stickers. Just paper clips, some rubber bands, and an envelope.

Ugh, just when I thought I was done shredding.

Wait, this one is addressed to *me*.

What is this? I've never seen this white security envelope before, with Dad's distinctive handwriting, obviously left for me.

I slowly start to open the envelope. This is such an incredible surprise. I never imagined I would hear my dad's voice or read his thoughts ever again. And here I am, about to uncover something he's addressed to me and only me. And I absolutely love that he *knew* I'd be the one to find this.

I look up to the ceiling and thank Dad for this amazing surprise. I have no idea what I am about to find out, good or bad. But having something my dad has left *just* for me is beyond special. Let me close the door. All I need now is for Cozette to burst into the room and take away this special moment.

Once the office door is closed, I can faintly hear the front door opening, Joe walking in, and Cozette squealing, followed by his husky voice asking for stromboli.

I get back on my feet slowly, as both legs are now stinging with pins and needles from sitting in the same position entirely too long. I crack the door enough to greet Joe and to avoid the slim chance of him coming up.

"Hi Joe! I'm so glad you came! Let me just finish up these last few things, and I'll be down. I don't need your help up here, so get yourself some stromboli!" I yell from upstairs and make sure to get him off the hook before he feels obligated to come up and help me.

I'm pleasantly surprised he came, and his timing is not ideal, but he seems appeased with food until I am finished reading what's in this envelope.

I get myself comfy in Dad's reclining office chair as I prepare to read. What could he possibly have to say? Why only to me? How did he know I'd ever find this? One million questions are swirling through my head. And I know reading this will answer most, if not all, of them. But I feel like I'm moving in slow motion. This is it. A rare moment I didn't expect to get with my dad, and I want to freeze time for as long as I can.

CHAPTER 11

MARTY

Timing has never been my strong suit.

I pull up to Helen's house and can't help but notice four cars in the driveway. Guess this lasagna won't last the three nights as I had hoped.

I walk up to the door, knock, and then just let myself in, as I always do.

"Did someone forget to invite me to the party?" I make light of the abrupt change from an intimate night to a family gathering.

"Oh, hi Marty, come on in! Have some stromboli; Kristy brought two, and they're enormous!" Helen yells from the kitchen.

I take off my shoes and hang my coat on the front chair in the living room.

"I guess we can save this piping hot, homemade lasagna for tomorrow night, then. I figured you were getting sick of creamy casseroles and could use a little variety. And I brought your favorite for dessert!"

"Not chocolate ice cream?!" she asks, giddy as a schoolgirl.

"Not *just* chocolate ice cream... No ice cream sundae is complete without...?" I tease.

"Wet walnuts! How did you remember?!" A smile spreads from ear to ear across her face.

Helen seems very pleased to see me, or maybe it's the walnuts.

Either way, it's nice to see her smile. Cooking for herself is probably the last thing she wants to do these days. I remember her saying during one of our family dinners that if it were up to her, she'd have appetizers, dessert, and a cocktail every night and skip the main course altogether. But her family expected dinner, so she would make them a full meal with protein every night. She was half joking, I assumed, but I know from experience that cooking for one can be depressing. She needs to eat a more well-rounded diet; desserts and cocktails won't sustain her for very long.

"Sure, I'd love some stromboli. Hey Joe, hi Sandra. How are you two holding up?"

They mumbled something to the effect of "fine" and "okay." So I turned my attention to Helen.

"I came to bring you dinner, but more importantly, I want to help."

"Help with what, Marty?"

This trip was actually just as much for me as for Helen. I was hoping tonight I would get a little snooping in. That's not happening now. It would've been hard enough with just Helen's eyes on me. Now I certainly won't get away with anything with the kids here, too. Maybe next time.

"I know you've been struggling with the task of cleaning things out, like Tom's office, so I want to do it for you. Won't take no for an answer."

I want to be sure Helen knows that this is a statement and not a question.

"That is very kind of you, Marty, but Kristy has beaten you to it. She has been spending a lot of time up there, sorting through files and shredding. I think she is just about done."

My facial expression shows disappointment that I can't hide. So instead of "taking no for an answer," I just excuse myself and head upstairs.

These carpeted stairs are perfect for sneaking up on someone, if you want to. The wooden stairs in my home give away each and every step taken.

I crack the door of the office open to see Kristy sitting in Tom's chair, opening a letter with such a look of determination on her face, I can't help but be intrigued.

"Whatcha doin'?" I obviously startled Kristy.

"Jesus, Marty! You scared me to death. What the hell are you doing here!?"

"I'm here to help!" I say, expecting a much warmer reception.

"If you wouldn't mind, Marty, I'd like to be alone. I'll come down when I'm finished."

"Are you sure there is nothing I can help you with? We could get through this twice as fast with some extra hands. And I could be helpful with any work things that are found—they should probably be read through to see what's important before getting tossed."

I would really like to be included in this clean-out, but Kristy is not thrilled to see me.

"No, Marty, please just go back downstairs. I'd like to do this myself."

Damn.

It's written all over her face. Kristy is hiding something.

CHAPTER 12

KRISTY

Although I'm sure he's trying to be helpful, Marty is nothing but in the way right now. And for some reason, he hasn't been taking no for an answer without several attempts at getting what he wants. It's exhausting.

I resume my comfortable position in Dad's chair and begin to open the envelope addressed to me. Checking the door one last time, hoping to read this in its entirety, without yet another interruption.

"Hey Kiddo! If you are reading this, either you are snooping in my office, or sadly, you are cleaning it out. If I know you—and I do—it's probably the latter. I am hoping that I am at a ripe old age and that Cozette is married with children. If not, and I have met my demise sooner, then I am especially glad that I am writing this letter to you.

I'm sure this is completely unexpected. Let me start with this. Ever since the day you were born, you have been the light of my life. Of course, I adore your brother and sister equally as much. But you and I always shared a special bond. We knew what the other was thinking at the dinner table with just a look. We could finish each other's sentences, especially, and most importantly, in charades! We excelled at every family game night and whooped the family's butts with our wit and smarts. And we shared the same opinion on just about everything. Except fluff. Who even eats that?

The sticky mess it creates, the ripped-up bread it leaves behind, and the sugar content that no human should ingest at a meal are just a few reasons. But I digress.

You three, Mom, and Cozette know how much I love you—more than anything in this world. You also know I would do absolutely anything for you.

Which leads me to this note and the final game we can play together. We always shared a love of puzzles and games, and I'll finally admit, you are more skilled than I! The student has become the master!

Follow these simple clues (simple for you, impossible for most...)

And I think you'll be extremely happy that you did.

I know you remember what we planted for Mom on Mother's Day when you were little. If you go there, you may get a better understanding of this game.

And if Cozette is still little, I just know Mom would take such pleasure in staying with her while you're gone. She brought such joy to our lives and made us feel young again!

A granddaughter is the greatest gift we could have ever been given. Thank you for that.

*And thank you for being an incredible child who has grown into an
equally incredible adult. You made parenting easy and the best job
in the world.*

OOO, Dad"

This is clearly a dream. But if it is, I'm sure I wouldn't be hearing
Cozette's giggles from Uncle Joe acting as the tickle monster. And I
wouldn't be smelling the stromboli heating in the oven. And this letter
wouldn't be signed, OOO. Dad was a big hugger; all the Shores are big
huggers. And my dad would say, "If one O is a hug, then three O's is a
really long hug." This is not a dream; I'm wide awake.

What is this letter all about? Was my dad losing his marbles as he aged?
I have many questions, and he seems to think Mom's favorite maple tree at
our old house will have the answers.

First things first, I'll go downstairs to see if anyone else has found
letters addressed to them left behind by Dad. Wait, that may not be the
best idea. What if he hasn't? He did mention our bond. Maybe this is for
me, and me alone? Do I share with them what I've found? Do I go to the
maple tree and see if there are any answers? Maybe that's the way to go.
Head over to the house we lived in when the three of us were little, then
I'll understand what's going on, and *then* I'll talk to the family about this
letter I've discovered.

I had better get downstairs before they come up, fearing I've drowned
in paperwork, intending to save me. Or worse yet, Marty comes back
trying to be helpful, and I'll need to awkwardly kick him out again. I try to
get myself together as I descend the fourteen stairs and make my way
around the hall to the kitchen.

"Hey, guys!" I manage to muster my calmest voice possible.

"Hey Kristy! Thanks for dropping the hint about stopping at Shamrock on your way over. That made my decision to come over a lot easier."
Joe has never had a filter; he just says whatever is on his mind. Mom likely
thought he was coming over to see her. Sadly, to find out now that the
stromboli was the driving force behind his decision.

"Sweetie, I can't thank you enough for cleaning up Dad's office for me. That was one project I really don't think I could've gotten through in less than six months," admits Mom.

"Well, it's not exactly cleaned up completely. I still have his desk to attend to. But I thought it was time for a break. You're not converting that room into, like, a gym or anything, are you?"

"Oh gosh, no! I just wanted to make sure there wasn't anything time-sensitive in there that needed attention. Dad paid all the bills, so I certainly don't want there to be any lapse in payments."

"Oh, Helen, I can definitely help you with that. I always took care of the bill paying in my house. I don't mind it at all, I'd love to help," Marty proudly exclaims.

"Good, so there's no rush in finishing it up," I say, relieved.

Ideally, I'll get Cozette to preschool tomorrow morning and rush over to the old house. It's killing me not to go tonight, but with daylight saving time, the Northeast gets dark by 4:30; it's quite depressing.

"Oh, okay," Mom adds, while wiping down the countertops in her otherwise immaculate kitchen. "You were up there awhile tonight, so I figured you wrapped it all up. But no, there's no hurry, and I'm certainly not turning it into a gym. It'll be my sewing room, since it has such great natural lighting. And I really can't thank you enough for doing this for me."

"No problem. Hey! Joe, did you eat *all* the stromboli?"

"No, I saved you a little; it's in the oven, staying warm. But if you don't eat it soon, I'm finishing it." Joe isn't kidding. If it's not nailed down or claimed, he'll devour it.

With my head in the oven, I think it best to gently inquire, without giving away my findings, "Do you guys wonder if Dad had any unfinished business? I mean, everything happened so fast. But I'm sure he would've left us letters or something had he known it was his last day. Don't you think?"

Sandra looks up at me while playing on the floor with Cozette; she really is the most attentive aunt ever. "Umm, have you lost your mind? I think too much time in Dad's office alone has caused you to go batty. No,

I do not think Dad would have left us letters. I think if he knew it was his last day with us, he would've sat us all down and told us everything he wanted us to know. And as far as unfinished business... what did he do besides go to work, buy lottery tickets, and play with Cozette? Nothing that I can think of, so I'm guessing no unfinished business either."

Well, I think I have my answer from Sandra. Between that answer, Joe's lack of filter or discretion, and Mom's inability to keep a single nugget of information to herself, I think it's evident that I'm the only one who's received a letter.

I finish up my dinner and scoop up my keys. "Alright, Cozette, give some goodbye hugs; we must get you home to bed. And you can pick which *lovie* you want to pack for school tomorrow!"

Acting as if it's a fun game of showing off her collection of stuffed animals, one by one, has been a pretty good distraction. I really do need to locate Fudge. Or work more hours to finally suck it up and buy a new one.

But for right now, I need to get home. Tomorrow cannot get here fast enough.

CHAPTER 13

MARTY

I catch Kristy in the foyer, struggling to get Cozette's arms into her pink, puffy coat.

"Hey Kristy, before you go, can I talk to you for a second?"

I've been debating this since Tom's death. I need to share with the kids what Tom has shared with me. It's only fair.

"Umm, yeah, but I really need to get Cozette home before she falls asleep." A less than enthusiastic Kristy answers, standing by the front door, her hand now on the doorknob, ready to leave.

"I can walk you out to your car if you'd like. It's better if we are away from curious ears anyway." Kristy stays put.

"So, I wanted to talk to you about your mom. And I thought it best to talk to you as the oldest, and you can relay the information to your siblings as you see fit."

"Marty, you're scaring me. What are you talking about?"

I seem to have Kristy's attention now, as she drops her hand from the doorknob and looks into my eyes intently.

"Your dad shared with me some information about your mom's health right before he passed. As it turns out, she has been diagnosed with early-onset dementia. It's obviously still in the very early stages."

I break the news to Kristy, knowing it's not my place and wishing I didn't have to.

"Marty, what are you talking about? As people age, they start forgetting things. You can't tell me you always remember where you put your keys. I think you're exaggerating a bit."

"Well, I clearly have no reason to exaggerate. I am just making you privy to a conversation your father had with me recently."

I can't help but notice a chip that Kristy has on her shoulder with me tonight.

"Cozette, go give Grams another hug. I'll be one more minute, then we'll head home."

"What exactly did my father say?" she asks in a hushed tone, cautious as not to attract the attention of her family, two rooms away.

I sense that she is starting to believe me.

"Your dad has been concerned with your mom's forgetfulness and mood swings lately. Not to mention her erratic sleep patterns. They went to visit a neurologist to have some tests done."

"What? When? Why didn't he tell me?" Kristy's voice is getting more accusatory with each word, like I'm the bad guy here.

"He didn't want to worry you three. And he obviously thought he'd have more time. Time to talk with you himself. But under the circumstances, I'm sure he would have wanted me to tell you, so that you can keep an eye on her."

"I'm sure Mom has all these details. She doesn't seem the slightest bit concerned. I'm hoping you are making more of this than it really is. But thank you for sharing it with me. Do you know the physician they saw? I'll reach out to them and get the details from the doctor."

"I don't. But it will be easy enough for me to find out without involving your mother. I'll text you tomorrow. And Kristy? Just so you know, your dad was very worried about your mom's health. Especially because, like you said, your mom doesn't seem the slightest bit concerned. That is very common with dementia patients. Mental decline, confusion, and the inability to recognize obvious things are concerns."

Kristy mumbles something under her breath and collects Cozette to head home.

I did my part. I shared what I know. I tried to emphasize how serious this really is. It's up to her now to handle it however she chooses.

CHAPTER 14
KRISTY

Information overload.

I don't know how many more surprises I can handle.

Good or bad.

I really don't think I slept more than a couple of hours last night. Way too much swirling around in my head to be sleeping.

I will take Marty's information with a grain of salt until I get to the bottom of Mom's medical situation. Although Marty means well, sometimes I feel like he just wants to cause drama and make things a bigger deal than they really are. Never having had kids of his own, and with the loss of his wife, he has a lot of free time on his hands. And he also thrives on attention, which last night's conversation certainly got him.

Before talking to my mom, I will speak with the neurologist about the best way to handle this. Then I will discuss it with my siblings so we're all on the same page. For now, it's just innocent forgetfulness on my mom's part, nothing more.

I can hear Cozette stirring in her bed while I stare out the window at the soft drizzle that just began falling from the puffy, gray clouds. I am completely lost in thought. I have a few minutes before getting Cozette up and ready for preschool. So, I sit, and I think.

Wow. Just wow.

This message from my dad might just be the most interesting and exciting thing that has ever happened to me in my whole life. This letter I am holding has really taken the sting out of my dad's passing. Not to say I still don't feel, at times, unbearable sadness, because I do. But the thought that my life with my dad on this earth isn't yet over is something I wouldn't think possible in my wildest dreams.

Now to get Cozette up and ready. And most importantly, to pick out her stuffed animal du jour. I think she may be onto my distraction scheme. She has less and less interest in showing off new animals each day and more and more questions about when she can get Fudge back.

Now the questions have turned to, "Is Poppy bringing Fudge when he comes back?" This is getting trickier and trickier.

To my surprise, I go into Cozette's room to see a fully dressed little girl, in mixed and matched everything, from her head down to her shoes. And I am not changing a single thing. I wonder what kind of looks I'll be getting from all the snooty moms at drop-off. Sometimes I wonder if they are all in a secret competition of whose kid owns the most Lululemon and Vineyard Vines. I was not asked to be in said competition.

Finally, a little teddy bear, named aptly Tee Boo—because "teddy bear" is just too hard to say as a toddler—was picked as the winner of the day. He was so loved from birth to age three, before those dreaded Real Dog commercials began. Tee Boo will do just fine, even with his one eye and thread for a nose where a button used to be, sewn back on more times than I can count.

I feel like our morning is moving as slowly as the thick syrup I poured on Cozette's party pancakes at breakfast. Putting Jimmies in pancake mix makes any breakfast a party, and, at this point, I will do whatever it takes for this kid to leave the house with a smile.

We ran to my car, dodging raindrops. Am I the only person on the planet who doesn't own a single umbrella that isn't broken? I managed to cut three fingers this morning, while the ribs of each umbrella took on lives of their own.

Looking ahead as we drive to school, I see the clouds breaking up and sunshine trying desperately to reveal itself. Fortunately, it doesn't look like we will need umbrellas much longer today, after all.

Drop-off complete. An uneventful drop-off is the best kind of drop-off because my life has been anything but uneventful lately.

My car, as if on autopilot, heads straight toward my childhood home. Hitting every single red light, it takes a total of twelve minutes until I arrive. Not sure I took a single breath during that entire twelve-minute stretch.

I park on the street, directly across from my old home. Looking at this house brings immediate chills to my arms. The aluminum siding has been painted light gray from the mustard yellow it was when we lived here. And the window shutters are now black, painted over the brown that I remember.

What an amazing house to be raised in. Not big, but as intimate and homey as they come.

Something tells me that no matter where we grew up, my mom would have found a way to make it intimate and cozy. I bet it still smells like a coniferous tree inside. At least that's how I remember it.

Christmas holds the best and most vivid memories for every kid. And for me, that includes the smell of our freshly cut Fraser fir Christmas tree we decorated each year.

As I walk up the driveway to the backyard, I expect I'll have some explaining to do to the current owners. To my surprise and relief, no cars are in the driveway, which means there's a very good chance that no one is home. This is great, because I didn't even rehearse what I planned to say to them. "Umm, yeah. Mind if I snoop around your backyard for a bit? What am I looking for, you ask? Dunno. But I should be off your property in no time, thanks!"

It appears there are no cameras or doorbell eyes watching me. So aside from a possible nosy neighbor, I may be in the clear.

Huge exhale.

I walk around the house to the yard, and I'm surprised to see how much it's changed. It takes me aback to see all that is different. The lawn, once of clover and zoysia, has now become lush, emerald, carpet-like grass. Although beautiful, I miss the fresh smell of clover that would overwhelm my senses as soon as I turned the corner. Now, what isn't covered in lush, verdant grass is newly laid pavers in exquisite patterns. This yard looks like something out of a magazine.

My sense of smell has always been exceptional, and this yard was always full of different scents. I chalk my great nose up to my horrible eyesight. It was all but a guarantee that, at an early age, I would need glasses. Every single member of my immediate family has been wearing glasses or contacts for as long as I can remember. I often wish I had inherited my mom's straight hair instead of her 20/150 eyesight. What's the saying? Lose one sense, and another gets heightened? Well, that's my sense of smell. Heightened.

My contact lens-filled eyes lock on the maple tree. Wow, it has gotten big. I remember planting it with my dad and the disappointment on my face that I just couldn't hide. "What's wrong, sweetie pie?" I remember him asking me like it was yesterday.

Holding back tears, I told him that I didn't want to get Mom a tree. I wanted to get her "Channel 5 perfume," as I called it, from Fastow's 5 and 10 store on Main Street. He assured me that a maple tree, Mom's favorite, was the best gift we could give her. He set the stage for every Easter and Mother's Day, when we would all stand in front of the tree for family photos.

And one day, in the very distant future, I'd stand with my date heading to the prom, in front of this tree, for photos. The visual he gave me was indisputable, even for a preschooler like me. True to his word, this tree served as the backdrop to just about every family pic.

But now it holds a much more important job. Hopefully, to answer many of my questions. But where do I begin? What am I looking for?

It is a beautiful December morning, and the skies have been uncommonly calm so far this autumn. Just about every maroon and coral leaf is still hanging on its limb.

I study the tree, wondering if it's supposed to speak to me. I half expected Dr. Seuss's Lorax to rise from the ashes and tell me what to do next. No such luck.

Dad can't expect me to dig through the dirt bed under the tree, can he? How long ago was he here? When did he leave me this clue? We have likely seen rain or snow since he's been here, so he wouldn't have left something that could wash away. It must be on the actual tree. I start to inspect. Nothing, from what I can see.

This has always been a great climbing tree with limbs in perfect positions for little ones to be a few feet off the ground but feel as though they were eight stories high. I decide to climb.

I only get to the first split of the tree before I realize my feet were much smaller the last time I attempted this climb. God, it must have been over twenty years since I climbed this tree, or any tree for that matter.

As I stand there, suspended in midair, about eighteen inches off the ground, I look up to scour the bark above. That's when I see it. Some kind of engraving in the tree limb above. I can't make out what is carved unless I get a little higher. Could this be it? This climb is much harder than I remember. I make it to the second large limb, eye level to the carving. No question, this is my dad's writing.

But what on earth does it mean? "Pic #1 OOO" That is it. Just Pic #1 OOO. Dad is the only person I ever knew to write the number one without the line on the bottom. Sometimes it even resembled a number seven more than a one. There is no denying that this is from my dad. "OOO," his signature sign-off, as confirmation. I look around for more; this can't be what he wanted me to see. I don't even get it. Has the rest weathered away?

I snap a pic with my phone, if nothing else, for the mere nostalgia of seeing my dad's distinctive writing. Albeit it's only eight characters.

Defeated, I climb down as my feet begin to fall asleep, squeezed between the tiny nook of the limbs. Sitting on the freshly laid mulch under the tree, I try to figure out what this could possibly mean. After a few minutes, I think better of it and go back to my car.

Why tempt fate by sitting in this stranger's backyard when I can just exhale in my car and brainstorm what this clue could possibly stand for?

After brushing off the dirt on my jeans before getting into my freshly washed car, I sit to think.

The only Pic #1 that has any relevance to me or my dad would have happened right at that tree. Is he referring to the first picture we ever took as a family in front of it?

Okay, well, that could be easy enough. Let me just think back. What year would that have been? We moved out, during my junior high years, from this three-bedroom house to a four-bedroom. So, we left here when I was twelve, Joe was seven, and Sandra was five. We bought the tree for Mom on Mother's Day after Sandra was born. She was born on August 16th, so the first family photo in front of the Mother's Day tree could have been that summer, or possibly my first day of school...

Back to Mom's I go!

But first I'll need to call some coworkers to see who can take my lunch shift. The list of people I need to pay back is getting longer and longer.

Considering I am running out of favors with my coworkers, this could take me a while.

CHAPTER 15

"Hi honey, it's me. I miss you. Can you meet me at my mom's after work? I have a fun project for you to help me with." I practically sing on Leo's voicemail.

I'm thinking he will be so intrigued to join me with the vaguest of details.

I head right to Mom's from our old house.

I feel so happy and content knowing that Dad did this for me. It shows me that he loved our days of playing detective games and doing puzzles as much as I did. A form of closure, perhaps. But whatever his intent, it's working.

My college roommate and best friend, Amy, once told me that I'm really good at three things.

Or maybe she said I'm *only* good at three things.

Either way, those three things, in no particular order, are first dates, job interviews, and scavenger hunts. Random, I know. But one of my only three talents is certainly going to come in handy right now.

I pull up to Mom's with a little less than an hour to spare before having to pick up Cozette.

I can get through many photos in all Mom's unlabeled albums if I don't run into any distractions. If I can't find the photo I'm looking for—in front of the maple—at least I'll have Leo to help me later this evening, which sounds so much more fun anyway. Plus, Cozette misses him. When Leo is not around, she asks where he is. And when he is around, she hangs all over him. A big, fun playmate.

We have all been so preoccupied for many different reasons since Dad died. We need more structure and routine, especially Cozette. Kids thrive on routine, and I haven't been able to give her much of that these past few weeks. Leo and Cozette adore each other, so tonight will be good for everyone involved.

By the time I finish explaining to Mom that I would like to reminisce through her photos and that Leo is coming over to join me, it's practically time for aftercare pickup, zero albums opened.

Nothing can be casually said in passing around here. It's always, always followed up with questions. Who, what, where, when, and why?

I should have added the Q&A to my timeframe. I know better than that by now.

Being vague can be hard for a wordy person like me. "No, Mom, no reason. I just want to show Leo some old pics."

Leo replies exactly as I suspected he would: *"K."* Man of few words and very predictable. Two of the many reasons we are so good together. Two *wordies* in one relationship can be a bit much.

We both pull up to Mom's at the same time, as if he were waiting at the corner for me. Wait, was he? Anyway, it is so good to see him! It's only been days, but it feels so much longer.

Cozette practically jumps out of my arms when she sees him. There is no better feeling than being on the receiving end of a toddler running toward you, smiling ear to ear, arms open wide, ready to be caught. After Cozette releases Leo's neck from her tight embrace, we head inside.

"Are you going to tell me about this little project I'm here to help you with?" he asks.

"Well, let's just go inside and get Cozette settled with Mom, then we'll head down to the basement, and I'll fill you in. There is quite a bit we need to catch up on. But let's wait until we're out of earshot." That should be enough information to pacify him for now.

"Hi Mom, we're all here!" I yell as I open the door. It still smells of Frasier fir and Stove Top stuffing yumminess. Cooking or not, she always manages to keep the aroma of family gatherings. I wish there were some way to bottle this scent.

"Come in, come in, I'm so happy to see you three! I've had a lonely day of no company and just cleaning bathrooms." The guilt trip begins.

"I stopped to pick up dinner for Cozette. Pretty sure she's all casseroled out." I place the takeout bags on her Formica countertop. "If you want to just play with her for a bit after she eats, she'd love it, and Leo and I can go to the basement and look through some albums." More of a statement from me than a question.

I drop my purse and keys and lead Leo downstairs.

For a neat freak like Leo, the sheer number of items in this basement can be overwhelming. I'm trying to hide the hoarding tendencies that I've inherited from my mother until after we are engaged. No need to scare him off before I even get a ring.

His jaw drops to the floor, and he can't even get past the aisles of wrapping paper. My mom's collection of all things bows, bags, and paper can rival any Hallmark store. Oh, he hasn't seen anything yet; we haven't even turned the corner to the good stuff. Until you've witnessed the Tupperware stacked upon Tupperware of grade school art projects, you have not seen hoarding.

Leo is all but speechless when I take him by the hand and remind him why we're here. For a minimalist like himself, this is an overwhelming amount of "stuff." Without my few personal touches in his home, it would look like he was in the process of moving in or moving out. His home is as sterile as a hospital, with not a thing out of place. I give him a minute to compose himself.

The two of us can rummage through the photo albums, wherever they might be, and I will be able to explain my findings from last night. "Let's just focus on the albums. When we find them, we can split them up. We're looking for a specific photo." He has still not said a word but is looking at me like I am one hundred percent certifiable.

Around the corner, under the stairs, are the bookshelves. It seems like as good a place to start as any. Sure enough, among all her stacked mystery novels lie at least forty photo albums. I never appreciated Mom taking so many pictures when we were growing up. As a matter of fact, I hated it. We all did. Every one of us, including Dad, would complain.

But that didn't stop her. There she would be, clicking away on her disc camera, all smiles as if she didn't even hear us. And for that I am thankful. Because now we have all these memories, and possibly an answer to this mystery.

Before we roll up our sleeves and start looking, I explain in detail the letter I found last night. Now he, too, is intrigued. Maybe I should've opened with that. Explain the letter, and get an even more willing Leo to help. How do I not know my audience?

He reaches for an album even before I can.

I hear Cozette giggling upstairs at her favorite *Peppa Pig* show, so I know we are fine to be down here for a while.

"Remember, any pictures by the maple tree, and specifically when I am around kindergarten age," I explain again, just to be clear.

"You mean, like this one?"

CHAPTER 16

MARTY

I'm going to pay Helen a visit tonight.

Tom would want me to.

I am curious to see how she is holding up mentally. With her fragile condition and now her husband dying unexpectedly, she should be watched closely.

I forwarded Kristy Helen's doctor's contact information, as she requested. Which I am happy to do. I would much rather take care of Helen in the intimate setting of her home than worry about all of her inevitable upcoming doctor appointments.

The kids can deal with the logistics, and I'll take care of watching Helen closely and keep them informed of anything that seems off.

This will also give me more of a reason to just pop in.

There are only so many dinners a man can make. Plus, it's getting expensive to cook these big meals. My budget is used to a weekly shopping order of TV dinners and an occasional bottle of shampoo.

What is most intriguing to me is Tom's desk. I am very curious as to what kind of work he brought home from the office and what bills he has that may need tending to. And of course, his lottery tickets.

That will be my first order of business.

The least I can do for this family is to be there for their mother, who will be getting worse with time, not better. Tom saw me through my worst. First, not being able to have children of my own, and then the loss of my beloved wife.

"Work-wife" is such a common term. What is the term for a friend who is closer than a brother, that you tell everything to, and who knows your every secret? Well, whatever that word is, it's what Tom was to me, and I was to Tom.

No one cares or has sympathy for the work friend after a death. But Tom was more than that to me. He was family. And I should step in where he left off and take care of his family as he would have wanted me to.

CHAPTER 17

KRISTY

Leo hands me an old, yellowed photo.

"Oh my gosh! This is amazing!" I haven't even gotten the chance to open my first album, and he is already completely invested.

"I don't think this is the photo we're looking for, but what a great picture and a fantastic start!"

The picture Leo handed me is one of my favorite memories of Joe, Sandra, and me in front of the maple tree, holding our prizes from the local fall festival. But I must be eleven or twelve here, and not five or six.

Maybe I wasn't clear enough about what a five-year-old girl would look like? Am I naïve to assume Leo would know exactly what we're looking for? I laugh out loud. He is the smartest person I know, but when it comes to things like this, which I think are common sense, he lacks a bit. No fault of his own. He has four brothers and no sisters and obviously does not have a daughter. So really, what was I expecting?

"Let's keep looking. Try to envision me about half this age, okay? Maybe just a couple of years older than Cozette."

Can't help but giggle while I explain.

Hundreds of photos of uneventful days playing in the park or at the breakfast table. And some very memorable days of class trips, where Mom was always Homeroom Mom. Beach pictures and first-day-of-school pictures. Token pics of Dad on Father's Day opening his gifts of aftershave from Joe, rubber bands and red Sharpies from Sandra, and Gold Toe socks from me. We were so excited to give him our gifts that we wrapped ourselves, and he was so good at acting like he wasn't expecting those exact gifts.

None of these timeless pictures is what I am looking for, though. Once we find the maple tree picture, I will make a point to come down here and sort through some of these albums. But I'll do it when I have more time. Now I need to focus.

"Keep looking, Leo. We need to find the earliest ones from this house." About a half dozen books later, I find what seems to be the right timeframe. Our first full summer in our new house.

I know this is it, because it's the first year we belonged to the local swim club. We loved that pool so much. Every day was a new adventure. We would stay for over six hours a day and complain when we had to leave so Mom could have dinner ready when Dad got home from work. Such simple times.

This has to be the album. Of course, it's from Mom's birthday! How did I not think of that? We gave Mom the tree for Mother's Day, and her birthday always falls on Memorial Day weekend. I search for a shot of us in front of a three-week-old tree.

Bingo! There are many shots from this weekend in the album. But only one has clearly been removed and then put back in. The other pictures have all been stuck in their pockets, as if they had become one with the cellophane. But this one is unlike the others. I carefully remove it, as it has been protected by this book for thirty years. "Leo, this is it! I found it, I found it!" I get the same wave of excitement I did when I found Dad's first letter to me.

We inspect the picture and quickly turn it over, assuming there has to be more to this on the other side. Here it is, what I've been hoping to discover since climbing the maple tree. More of Dad's impeccable handwriting. But this time, it is so minuscule, it mimics typed print.

"Hey Kiddo!

*See! This is not going to be challenging for you at all. And quite possibly a little fun? You need to have more fun, Kristy. Life can be challenging and at times outright hard. But don't forget to let go on occasion and just BE. Here is a chance for you to just **BE**. Live in the moment and enjoy your life. You only get one. Let me say that again. ONE. So, take this one life of yours and live it the best you know how. Be kind. Have fun. And don't forget to look around and enjoy the sights from time to time.*

*Starting with where your mom and I began our beautiful life together as husband and wife. (I'll never forget, it was during the heatwave of '87. We had the **AC ON** the entire weekend!)*

OOO, Dad"

Leo and I read it again and again. Then we just stare blankly at each other.

"Well, obviously, I have no idea what that means, honey. I'm guessing you do?" Leo tries to cushion the blow when he sees the blank look on my face.

"No, I have absolutely no idea what this means. It wouldn't seem too difficult if not for the random bit about the heatwave and AC. And why the sporadic bold letters? Is that supposed to mean something? He took the time to get a Sharpie and bold those few words. That must mean something, right? I guess asking Mom where she and Dad began their life together would be a good start. But I was already at our first house in Haddonfield. Do you think he wants me to go back there?" I desperately shoot questions at a guy who literally just said he has no idea what my dad is talking about.

"I guess we should go talk to your mom about it. And it's suspiciously quiet up there; we should probably see what they're up to." Leo is always my voice of reason. And also, my anchor to reality.

Cozette. We've been down here for what feels like hours with zero interruptions. That *is* very suspicious.

We cautiously walk up the stairs, as quietly as we can, only to see the back of my mom and Cozette snuggled up on the couch, looking at picture books. What a beautiful sight.

After Cozette turns the last page, Leo lifts her out of the plush blankets and into his arms, and we say our goodbyes.

Mom looks up, very confused. "Mom, what's wrong?"

"I, I... what are you doing?" She stumbles to get her words out.

"We're taking Cozette home. She needs a bath, and then it'll be her bedtime. Why, what's up?"

"Oh, nothing. I think I just dozed off for a second. Sorry."

Wait. What?

It concerns me that Mom would fall asleep while watching Cozette, even if we *were* right downstairs. But what's even more concerning is that she wakes up with such a level of confusion, looking as though she doesn't even know where she is. That would be completely understandable if it were at a sleepover party or even on vacation. Waking up in an unfamiliar room can cause confusion, sure. But in her own living room, where she's lived for over twenty years?

Fortunately, Marty provided Mom's doctor's contact information, and I've already started the ball rolling on getting her records. I've sent the doctor's office two emails with what I think is all of the required information and Dad's death certificate. I've even signed the HIPAA request form. Now I anxiously wait to hear back from them to confirm this is just a case of waking up discombobulated mid-dream and not that Marty was actually onto something.

∽

Cozette's nighttime bath routine leaves her so relaxed that putting her to bed afterward takes very little effort. Tonight was no exception. Now Leo and I are able to spend the rest of our night however we like.

We should take this newfound free time to start a Netflix show that everyone has seen, except us. Or maybe we can play Scrabble. Or maybe, and most likely, we'll jump into bed and just enjoy each other.

"Hey, honey," I hear Leo announce from the bedroom. "I know it's really early, but I'm going to call it a night, too. I have to do a presentation for some important clients early tomorrow morning, and I want to review it quickly before bed."

"Oh, okay. Goodnight then. I won't be in bed for a while; I'm not tired yet. Love you!"

"Love you too."

With that, my plans for this evening have changed.

Well, since I'll have to wait to talk to Mom until tomorrow, I should start a list of possible places Dad could want me to go next. It couldn't be where they met or had their first date. The picture specifically said, "Began our life as husband and wife." Could he mean where they honeymooned? And why can't I remember where that was? Well, I am certainly not going to solve this right now without Mom's assistance.

I hear the shower water turn on as I get cozy on the couch under my blanket to check my email.

"Ugh, thirty-two new messages!" I complain to myself. I'm assuming a majority are junk. Annoying, because I feel like I just cleaned out my inbox an hour ago.

After deleting the first nine junk emails, number ten catches my eye: *"Virtua Neurosciences—Advanced Neurologic Care—URGENT."*

CHAPTER 18

MARTY

Tonight is the night.

I'm as ready as I'll ever be—showered, shaved, and even applied a little Brut aftershave. I hope it doesn't overpower my Fahrenheit cologne.

By the time I'm primped and ready to go, I fear Helen will already have eaten dinner.

So, I do the next best thing and stop at the supermarket for angel food cake and ice cream.

Ding-dong.

Not sure why I always ring the doorbell. I don't usually wait for her to answer before letting myself in.

"Helen!? Are you here?"

"Helen?"

Where could she be?

I let myself in and explore the first floor.

No Helen.

"Helen, I'm coming up!"

I give her a fair warning, but her not answering has me concerned. I'm not leaving without seeing her.

When I get to the top of the landing, I can hear her rustling around in one of the bedrooms.

"Helen? Is everything OK? I brought you ice cream, and it's melting." I try to sound lighthearted, even though I'm feeling concerned and nervous at the same time.

"Oh, hi Marty! I didn't hear you come in! What are you doing here? It must be almost 8 p.m.!"

"Oh, hey! I've been calling your name. I didn't want to startle you. Just stopped by to see how you're feeling, and I don't know, take out your trash or whatever you need."

Of course, my reason is to hopefully snoop a bit more, acting like the helpful friend who's just looking for a spoon in all the drawers until I find what I'm looking for...

"That's very nice of you, Marty. I don't think I need anything. I was just sitting here folding some laundry. I've turned Sandra's room into a makeshift linen closet of sorts. There is so much more space in here. So, this is where I keep my freshly laundered towels and sheets, but sadly, since I'm the only person here now, I can go over a week between loads of laundry."

Beep, beep, beep, her phone notification goes off *again and again.* Good God! Her oldest daughter must text her twenty times a day! So annoying. I'll put a stop to that while I'm here. I need to focus, and these beeping interruptions are killing me.

"Hey, show me the latest pictures of Cozette!" I ask enthusiastically.

"Oh, of course! Here are some from when I watched her last week. I made her spaghetti for lunch, and she is wearing it all over her hair and face! Not to mention her outfit! And don't get me started on the floor, but she is just precious!" Helen beams with delight.

"May I?" I ask while reaching for her phone.

"Of course, flip through!"

I really couldn't care less about pictures of Cozette. What I *do* care about, though, is turning off this ringer of hers. There. Done. Simple.

Now I can expect a quiet evening, where I can accomplish what I came to do. And if I don't find any tickets, at least I will have a better lay of the land and will have an idea of where to search during my next solo visit.

I hand her back her phone, and we sit quietly on the spare bed.

This is my time. This is it.

I need to make my move before my nerves get the best of me.

I sit next to her on the bed and put my arm around Helen for comfort. To my delight, she lays her head on my shoulder.

I lean in and take her all in before I tenderly kiss her.

CHAPTER 19

Helen leans into my kiss as I hoped she would.

Just like old times.

And yet, I feel like this is better than old times. No longer will she need to sneak away to my home under the falsehood of "grocery shopping" or a "quick trip to Target."

As I lay her back gingerly on the bed, she hesitates.

"Marty, don't you think it's too soon?" Helen questions.

"I really don't. I've been wanting to get back to our lives before the accident. I don't think there is any kind of strict timeline on this."

"I know, I want it to be like it was also, but I think we need to wait a bit longer."

Frustrated, I get up off the bed.

"I understand, Helen. You just let me know when you're ready. I'll be here for you until then."

"Thank you for understanding, Marty. I do miss our intimacy, but my emotions are all over the place right now. Thank you for being patient with me."

With the ice cream melting on the counter, I let myself out.

CHAPTER 20

KRISTY

"Virtua Neurosciences—Advanced Neurologic Care."

This is the response I've been waiting for.

"Ms. Shore,

Attached are the most recent progress notes from your mother's office visit.

Based on our evaluation, including cognitive assessments, imaging studies, and neurological exams, we have identified signs consistent with early-onset dementia. There is progressive neurodegeneration affecting areas of the brain responsible for memory, reasoning, and daily function, occurring at an earlier age than typical late-onset dementia. The changes we see suggest that this is not just normal aging but rather a pathological process that will gradually impact cognitive and functional abilities over time.

Damn.

I was really hoping Marty's information was not accurate.

I am going to visit Mom today. Depending on her mood, I will bring this up and then call her provider to be sure I have all of her upcoming doctor's appointments on my schedule.

Modern medicine really is incredible. I hope they can prescribe some miracle medication to slow any, or all, of her mental decline.

~

After another rushed morning, we get Cozette off to school, and Leo heads out to work. Now my day can begin. I drive to Mom's without so much as a warning call to see if I can talk to her and find some answers. Fortunately, her car is in the driveway.

Two knocks to make her aware that she has company, then I let myself in.

"Mom, it's me. Where are you?"

"Oh, Kristy, what a nice surprise! I'm just in the kitchen watching *M*A*S*H* and eating my English muffin. What can I get you? A cupatea? I have honey for it."

"Sure, that'd be great!" I agree to tea more for her than for me.

Only Mom could turn three words into one. Cupatea. If someone were to come here with English as their second language, they would have a very hard time comprehending most conversations in this house. A cupatea to Mom just symbolizes quality time, not the beverage itself. You can see her whole body relax as I say yes to the tea.

I decide to just get right to it.

"Mom, how are you feeling?"

"I feel great, sweetie, why?"

"Well, I received an email from your neurologist. They sent notes from your most recent visit. I'm concerned about you."

"My neurologist? How on earth . . .? Why would they . . .? No, I assure you, I'm fine. They are just being a bit overcautious on my silly forgetfulness."

Mom explains first in a frustrated tone, then in a tone that quickly turns into her trying to reassure me.

"Okay, well, I guess it is good that they are being overly cautious. At least they are really on top of things. Just keep me posted on all of your upcoming appointments, okay?"

"Fine. But I assure you, it's not necessary."

Her frustrated tone is back.

I'm super anxious to continue my quest. "On a different topic, why can't I remember where you and Dad went on your honeymoon?"

"Oh, wow, I haven't thought about that trip in ages!"

I know better than to expect Mom to answer with just, well, the answer. I will certainly get the info I came for, but it will cost me a lot of reminiscing.

Which is fine, because today I need to remind myself that I have nothing but time. My shift at work isn't until dinner, so I don't need to head out until pickup time for Cozette. And I promised her an early pickup with Chick-fil-A for dinner, so I don't even need to think about a home-cooked meal.

"Let's see, we got married in the chapel at St. Rose. I'm sure I told you. We were on a budget, you know. Your dad wasn't as excited about a church wedding as I was, so we compromised and agreed to have our wedding in the chapel, where a priest was able to perform our marriage."

"Yes, Mom, I remember that story, but what about your honeymoon? Did you go on one?"

"Well, honeymoons then weren't like they are now. Most of my friends went to the Poconos for the weekend, and some ventured to Niagara Falls. But not us. Dad knew how much I adored Cape May, so he took me to a wonderful bed and breakfast less than a block from the beach!

"I remember how perfect it was. A beautiful, vintage Victorian home, built in the 1800s. We took carriage rides and had some wonderful dinners. And the shopping! Oh, the shopping! Some of my favorite stores are still there—such unique and wonderful stores! And they were right down the street from our bed and breakfast. That was my favorite vacation ever. And sadly, we never made it back to that B&B. You know how everything else becomes a priority when you have a family. Braces, school tuition, new shoes and clothes, sports, mortgage, bills... well, you can imagine. Needless to say, I wish Dad and I spent a little more time focusing on us and worried a bit less. But hindsight is 20/20."

I can see Mom's thoughts start to wander off, so I try bringing her back.

"That's such a nice memory, Mom. It's sad you and Dad never got back, but you can still go! What was it called?" I'm hoping Mom can at least give me the name of the B&B, so I don't have to flat out tell her why I'm asking. I planned to let her in on my secret quest, but something is telling me to wait. I just love having this small piece of Dad all to myself, and I want it to last a little longer.

"What *was* the name of that place? It was many, many moons ago. Gosh, I can't remember. But I do recall a lighthouse on the sign out front."

Okay, well, not the answer I was looking for, but it's a start. And after so many more stories of Cape May and the delicious Waldorf salad at Delaney's Pub, it was time for me to go.

"Thanks for the tea, Ma. I have to get going so I have time to shower before I get Cozette. Also, I'm picking up Chick-fil-A for you two for dinner. Same order?"

"That would be great, thank you. Looking forward to having Cozette over! I'll bring her home and have her in bed before you're done with your shift."

Music to my ears. I say it daily: I do not know what I would do without her.

The arrangement is really good for both of us. I get to work, and occasionally I can do things with Leo. And Cozette keeps Mom young and on her feet. There's no time to be lazy and wallow in self-pity when there's a curious three-year-old tugging on your pant leg, asking a million questions.

Fortunately for me, Mom is available no matter what my shift. And tonight, it may be a long one. I need to stay as long as they'll keep me. With my sporadic shifts lately, my funds are lower than usual.

～

After dropping Cozette and lots of chicken and waffle fries off at Mom's, I get back in the car to head to the restaurant. My phone beeps with a message from Leo. *"Hey, sweetie! I have been racking my brain trying to figure out your dad's message. I scrambled the highlighted letters and came up short. I was hoping to have an answer for you, but I got nothing. Unless 'cobane' or 'beacon' mean something to you or your mom, I'm back to square one. Text me after work so I know you got home safe. Love you."*

What a sweetheart. This is so not in his wheelhouse, but he's trying. And in his free time, nonetheless.

Although I'm not sure his efforts were fruitful. What is a "cobane" anyway? And isn't a "beacon" a fire? Or is it a light? Either way, I'm not sure it's exactly what I'm looking for.

I walk into work and hit the ground running. It feels like the Christmas season, and Christmas shopping starts earlier and earlier each year. With Christmas shoppers come post-shopping holiday eating and drinking. I barely have time to put on my apron before I'm taking orders.

I work at least three hours without so much as grabbing a sip of water or even saying hello to any of my coworkers. It isn't until hour four that I go to use the bathroom to clear my head.

Cobane. Beacon. Cobane. Beacon. Think!

I sit in the quiet and rack my brain before I head back out into the madness. I need to figure this out. I look up the definition of "beacon" on my phone. *"A fire or light set up in a high or prominent position as a warning, signal, or celebration."* That's exactly what a lighthouse has!

Beacon of light!

The light on top of a lighthouse! Could that be it?

Mom and Dad's B&B must have been named The Beacon.

This could be the next stop on this journey. I need to get back to my customers before they start getting angry and the tips start diminishing. This will have to wait.

But I do know one thing: we are going to take a little road trip to the Jersey Shore!

CHAPTER 21

After an exhausting shift and smelling like I've been rolling around in Old Bay and Miller Lite, I finally get to text Leo that I'm home. I long for the day when he can sell his house and move in with us, but until then, a goodnight text will have to do.

"Hi Mom, I'm home!" I managed in my quietest voice, as I could hear a pin drop, walking into my apartment.

Mom is snuggled up on the couch, and it breaks my heart to wake her. "Hey Mom, how about you sleep in my room, and I'll pull out the futon for me?"

"Oh, hi, honey! When did you get home? What time is it? Where are my glasses?" My discombobulated mother is not driving anywhere.

"I just walked in, but I don't want you driving home so late, especially after you've been sleeping. Seriously, go to bed in my room. I'm still wired from work and have some things to take care of on my computer. I'll wake you in the morning when I get home from dropping Cozette off at preschool."

"Oh, that sounds lovely." Mom barely opens her eyes as she feels her way to my bedroom. I doubt she will remember this conversation in the morning.

I *am* wide awake after being immersed in a lively, loud crowd for the last eight hours, so I might as well make good use of my time. I'll start by looking up B&Bs in Cape May. If Cape May is in fact the right place, I wonder what Dad could possibly have in store for me there?

Much to my disappointment, when I type in *"Bed and Breakfast in Cape May, NJ,"* nothing associated with a lighthouse, much less a beacon, appears. The Star Inn is the only B&B that has anything to do with light, and they just went through a renovation and were renamed in 2019.

Certainly not old enough to accommodate my honeymooning parents. I have to think of something else. I try typing in *"beacon"* to see what comes up.

First to appear is a building material supplier and an apartment building in Philadelphia. But wait. Down the list is exactly what I'm looking for! "The Beacon, the most beautiful Victorian rental on the coast of Cape May!" Now we're getting somewhere! Okay, so maybe it's not the B&B Mom remembers. But this must be it, right?

The very first description says it's *"located on the beach block and steps away from amazing shops and wonderful restaurants."* That is all Mom talked about. This *has* to be it! I'm reserving a room before I even talk to Mom.

Our first family vacation with Leo!

But as it turns out, I won't be reserving a room; I'll be reserving the house. Okay, this is more than I bargained for, but it can be done. After all, this Jersey Shore resort is probably gorgeous during the Christmas season. And fortunately for me, Cozette doesn't completely grasp the whole concept of Christmas presents. I can get away with the gifts I've already bought her; no need for more. The rest of my Christmas gift savings is going toward this house. And I think we would all agree, a vacation is very much needed right now.

I'd better text Leo so he reads it at 5 a.m. when he typically wakes up. That way, he can confirm that I'm not losing my mind and reassure me that going to Cape May this weekend is a good idea.

"Hi sweetie! It's after midnight, but you'll be getting this in a few hours when you wake up. What are your thoughts on a weekend getaway? Turns out, you were spot on with your BEACON letter scramble! I'll explain when I see you, but I booked two nights in Cape May for this weekend. Thinking Mom and Cozette may join us? Oh, and also, this is in lieu of exchanging Christmas gifts this year. Sorry!"

CHAPTER 22

Fortunately, Mom's lack of a social life allows for very last-minute weekend trips away. Which is great, because it would have been a waste of an entire house if just Leo and I had gone down alone. After all, we would have spent ninety percent of our weekend trip in the bedroom, which would feel a bit wasteful.

Instead, here we are, the four of us about to drive two hours to what could be a clue. A note from Dad? I really have no idea what I'm looking for. But worst-case scenario, we have a lovely weekend away together, and Mom can do some more reminiscing.

Getting Cozette packed and ready for a weekend away can be a challenge. With the number of things we need to pack for a toddler for two nights and three days, we might as well go away for a month. And the screaming doesn't help. Cozette has not forgotten about Fudge and begs me daily to find him. I've asked her to help by starting with her toy box. That will keep her busy while I pack the trunk, discovering all of the long-lost toys at the bottom of the box that she's forgotten about.

Leo walks in to see an unhappy Cozette, who is on a mission to find Fudge. The toy box was not the distraction I was hoping it would be.

When the car is packed up, I buckle Cozette in her car seat and get myself comfy in the front seat. As we are heading to pick up Mom on the way to Cape May, I can't help but sing Al Alberts's song with the same name.

Leo gets into the driver's seat and turns to Cozette with a Christmas bag filled to the brim with green and red tissue paper. "I know it's still about two weeks until Christmas, but I wanted to give Cozette her gift early. I think this is just as much a gift for us as it is for her," he says with a wink.

A Real Dog replacement! I disagree; this is *more so* a gift for Leo and me. She squeals with excitement, and she pulls it out of the bag. "Mommy, look, it's Fudge! And you changed her collar! It's pink, my favorite color!"

This is amazing. Leo is amazing. And now we can just about guarantee a peaceful ride to the beach.

This town looks as if it is a movie setting, just waiting to be filmed. Stunning and quaint at the same time. Each Victorian home is more gorgeous than the last. I can see why it holds such wonderful memories for Mom. Honeymoon or not, this place is like no other. And being decorated for Christmas takes it to the next level. What a fun weekend we are about to embark on!

My mind begins to wander as I hear Leo's navigation in her English accent, "Your destination is 1,000 feet on the right." Suddenly, chills rush through my body. I am so hoping we are at the right place, and I can see what Dad so desperately wants to share with me.

We pull into the extremely narrow driveway, which I can understand because real estate must be at a premium in this town. We don't have an inch to spare on either side, and as much as I want to run into the house and check it out, we seem to be driving in slow motion.

Once parked, I get a wiggly Cozette out of her car seat and check out the exquisite exterior of the home. Sure enough, every house is named, and this one is "The Beacon." The wooden sign on the front lawn, stating its name, is also adorned with a lighthouse!

This cannot be a coincidence. More chills.

Leo unpacks the car as Mom, Cozette, and I enter the code to the back door. Granted, I am used to and perfectly happy with my six hundred square feet, but this space is extraordinary. Huge, but still warm. Victorian with its beautiful, large, wooden floor planks, but modern with its kitchen appliances. The definition of the best of both worlds. Cozette is running around, checking out every nook and cranny. And there are many crannies and nooks. I look over at my mom as she stares blankly, tears filling her eyes.

"Mom?" I question, as I can't read her reaction.

"Kristy, this is the most thoughtful thing anyone has ever done for me. You said we were taking a little trip to Cape May, but I had no idea what you had in store! This is just incredible. This is the kitchen, albeit updated, where Dad and I came after shopping and grabbed lemonade before heading onto the front porch rocking chairs. How on earth did you find it?" an absolutely giddy Mom declares.

"Well, I was thinking we could all use a little time away. These past weeks have taken their toll on everyone. It's a shame Joey and Sandra couldn't join us. You did ask them, right?"

"Oh yes, I asked." Mom scowled. "Sandra has a weekend of bachelorette parties, and Joey didn't seem to think Leah would consider traveling with her mother-in-law a fun vacation."

So there's that. Mom has always had such a huge soft spot for Joey. Anyone in Leah's shoes would have an uphill battle with Mom. It must be challenging for Leah to always feel the need to prove she is worthy of her only son. But yikes, Joe. He should know better than to admit things like that out loud.

"Well, I for one am glad it's just us. It'll be nice to have quality time with Cozette, without the competition of her aunt and uncle. I have been very preoccupied lately. This weekend will be good for Cozette," I say to cushion the blow.

Around every corner, there is another unique bedroom. I decide to take the nautical room with Leo and give Mom and Cozette the larger bedroom at the back of the house. It has its own bathroom and a king bed to comfortably fit them both, even with Cozette's body shaped like an X while she sleeps.

Cozette has made it very clear that she is having a sleepover party with Grams tonight. She loves that Grams will read to her until she falls asleep. I, on the other hand, read one book, say goodnight, and leave the room.

Walking the cobblestone sidewalks, stopping to window shop, and looking at beautiful, soft, white Christmas lights that line the streets takes up the rest of the night. With, of course, a stop at Delaney's Pub, so Mom can get her Waldorf salad.

Mom wasn't kidding when she said their honeymoon accommodations were convenient to everything. Our location is perfect. It's just a short walk down Jackson Street to where The Beacon is located. Horses and buggies fill the streets, covered in Christmas lights and bells jingling. This place is almost magical, like out of a storybook.

We reach the house, and Mom and Cozette go in to start the bedtime routine, which I don't foresee taking very long. Cozette is exhausted.

Leo goes into the kitchen, and instead of coming out with lemonade, he emerges with two vodka and sodas.

Oh, how I love this man.

Is there anything more romantic than sitting on rockers on the front porch of a gorgeous Victorian home, watching all the many passersby and couples on carriage rides? I seriously doubt it.

Leo puts down my drink as I'm admiring the hotel across the street, covered in Santas climbing the exterior walls. "Leo, look at those amazing decorations! It's even more magical at night!" No reply.

"Leo?"

As I turn around, I don't see him at first. I don't see him because he is out of my direct line of sight. He is down on a bended knee.

He is down on a bended knee. He is down...

On bended knee!

Leo would not be so cruel as to joke about something like this, right?

Just as one million thoughts are swirling around in my head, he reaches into his pocket.

This is not a joke. It's happening. It is actually happening.

"Kristy Shore, I have been falling more and more in love with you since our first date. Watching you walk across the bar heading in my direction was the start of the happiest time of my life. I stood there for what felt like forever as you approached, thinking, *Please let this be her*. And when I went in for a handshake and you came back with, "Sorry, I'm a hugger," and brought me into your arms, I was a goner. That was the best first date, followed by the best day, every day after. I never want to have another without you. I will strive every day to make you and Cozette the happiest girls in the world. Will you make me the happiest man and marry me?"

This is the part where someone throws a glass of water in my face to wake me from my stupor. But it appears there is no water being thrown, and Leo is waiting for an answer.

"Yes! One thousand times, yes!"

CHAPTER 23

In the short time we have been here, I have realized something. Something is hiding in plain sight. This journey that Dad has me on, this fun hunt for what, I don't know. But even if there is no point or no prize at the end, this journey has been such a gift in and of itself.

Dad was a brilliant man. A man who knew his family and their needs more than anyone. Could Dad have sent me on this journey for *the journey?* I've been so fixated on what's next that I haven't truly appreciated the ride. But as I sit here and think about what Dad has given me thus far, the thought gives me chills. Never on my own would I have gone back in time to our perfect childhood house and climbed our maple tree. Never would I have taken Leo down into my mom's basement to look through album upon album of precious memories. Never would I have found myself, and my three most favorite people, in this fairytale place, to experience what Mom felt thirty-five years ago. And never would I have gotten proposed to in the most romantic way possible. I really do need to slow down and enjoy everything I have. Because, wow, am I blessed. Dad's words are really hitting hard right now.

"Live in the moment and enjoy your life. You only get one. Let me say that again. ONE. So take this one life of yours and live it the best you know how. Be kind. Have fun. And don't forget to look around and enjoy the sights from time to time."

Yes, Dad. I am going to do just that. Thank you for showing me the way, even after your life here on earth has ended.

~

As I make eggs for everyone this morning, in this gorgeous kitchen, I just can't stop smiling.

Leo seems to be all smiles too. What an incredible night we had together. I keep looking down at my left hand to glance at this stunning foreign object on my finger. He done good. We've never gone ring shopping, as I didn't want to take any of the romance out of it. I wanted to have and wear what *he* picked out for me, not what *I* researched, tried on, and chose myself. And I am so glad I did. Had I picked it out myself, I'm sure it would have looked just like this. I can't imagine anything looking more perfect for my hand.

I love that when I look at it, I can picture Leo in the jewelry store, nervously pacing about, going from one jewelry display to another. Questioning his decision until he found *The Ring*.

I snap back to reality when I hear Cozette and Mom talking like two little old ladies in their bedroom. "Grams, this place is far, but not as far as Costa Rica."

We've never been to Costa Rica. Have no plans to go to Costa Rica. And have never talked about Costa Rica. I love what comes out of that little girl's mouth. I can hear my mom ask, "What else do you know about Costa Rica?" And Cozette's very matter-of-fact answers, "My friend, Archie, at school went to Costa Rica for Thanksgiving, and it's even farther than Cape May." They are both giggling as they emerge from their room and into the kitchen.

I plan not to say a word until one of them notices the rock on my finger. Cozette bypasses me completely to make a dash for Leo. The look on her face tells me she forgot he was here. Their relationship makes me happier than anything in the world.

"Mmm, smells delicious! I thought we were going to the Mad Badder across the street for breakfast."

"Not this morning, Mom. We can go tomorrow. I decided to make Cozette's favorite dippy eggs this morning. Plus, Leo got up before the sun, and I didn't want him to have to wait to eat. But I made yours Benedict, the way you like them."

"Oh wow, I feel like this is a celebration of sorts. I never get my eggs Benedict unless I go to the Corner Bistro back home."

"Well, it's a great morning and a wonderful weekend. I thought I'd treat my favorite people to their favorite breakfasts!"

"My, aren't you extra cheery this morning?" Mom gives me a suspicious look.

Still, they haven't noticed. I had better join them at the table, or I may just burst.

I pull up a chair in the dining room next to Cozette and cut her toast in half.

"Mommy, so pretty!" she exclaims. "Can Cozette try?"

"Not this ring, sweetie. Mommy doesn't take this off."

Mom is so engrossed in her eggs Benedict that she is not even hearing these conversations. *Oh, for the love of God.*

"Mom, look!"

As Mom looks up from her plate, annoyed that I am interrupting her moment with her eggs, she sees my hand. "Kristy!" she squeals. "It happened!" She runs over to hug Leo, as she can't seem to take her eyes off my gorgeous, radiant solitaire rock.

She loves him. It's fine, I'll wait for my turn.

Meanwhile, Cozette is very confused. "Mommy, what's wrong with Grams? Why is she crying?"

"Nothing is wrong, sweetheart. Grams is really happy. So those are happy tears."

"Happy tears? At school, Mrs. Lauren says to wipe away our tears and get happy. Grams has it mixed up."

"Yes, I guess she does. Hey, how would you feel if Mommy and Leo got married, and the three of us all lived together?" I look intently at Cozette to see her true reaction to my question.

"Yay! Sleepovers every single night!" Cozette bursts.

There's my answer! I knew Cozette would be thrilled to have Leo around all the time, but it feels good to confirm my hope.

But equally as important is that, finally, Mom is trading her sad tears for happy ones, even if temporarily.

CHAPTER 24

MARTY

"Hi Helen! I hope you're enjoying your much-needed time away with Cozette and Kristy!"

I make sure to text Helen before letting myself into her house. Since I'm already in her driveway, I thought that texting her was a good idea. If I called to tell her I was dropping off food, she may tell me not to go out of my way or just to wait until she returns. I can't risk that. A text ensures no dispute. I can simply text, turn off my ringer, and ignore any reply.

"Just wanted to tell you to have fun and let you know I'm putting food in your refrigerator so you will have dinner waiting for you when you get home!"

Text sent. House keys in hand. Now comes the fun part.

What was Kristy hiding from me the other night? With any luck, I will find out right now.

After all, my last attempt at snooping was cut short by Helen rejecting my advances and my abrupt departure.

First things first, shoes come off so I don't accidentally track dirt all over the house. Then put the meatloaf and potatoes in the fridge.

Now, the reason for my visit.

After making room in the refrigerator, I quickly rummage through the junk drawers in the kitchen. Kristy may have taken whatever was in that envelope with her, but I am not at a dead end just yet.

Up to Tom's office to look through his desk. Specifically, to find the envelope Kristy was holding, hoping there was a chance she didn't take it with her. I would have assumed that if it was important, she would have, but I don't remember her carrying anything but a small purse when she left. I did get a good look at what she was holding as I was telling her about her mom's condition by the front door.

And there was no envelope in her hand.

Taking steps two at a time, my endurance is still as if I were twenty-four years old. I credit my active sex life to my cardiovascular excellence.

Going straight to Tom's office and taking a seat at his desk chair, I start with the drawers on my left—nothing but folders of taxes dating back over ten years. Interesting as this might be at any other time, these are not what I'm looking for right now.

But since I'm here, one peek won't take much time.

"What the hell!" I say out loud.

How could Tom possibly have made so much more than I do? Same job, same tenure, same responsibilities. Fuck!

I need to have a stern talk with my boss tomorrow morning.

Aside from the tax returns and a cigar box full of pill bottles, of which I recognize none of the medications, there is nothing of interest in any of these drawers, except for one manila folder with "*Doc Info*" written on the front of it. This could be interesting. Guessing it doesn't matter what medical info I know about Tom, now that he's gone. Possibly, it's more information on Helen's diagnosis.

There's only one way to find out.

Unlike the other opened envelopes and files, this one is sealed shut— sealed with adhesive *and* a metal clip. Now I am extremely intrigued.

I release the metal clip and slide my thumb under the adhesive. A rather thick stack of papers stares back at me, just waiting to be read. I pull the half-inch-thick pile out from the manila envelope, and immediately the heading on the first page grabs my attention.

BIOPSY RESULTS

"The results of your recent colonoscopy and subsequent biopsies have indicated a diagnosis of colon cancer.

We understand that this news may be unexpected and concerning, and we want to assure you that our team of specialists is here to provide you with the support and information you need. The pathology report indicates adenocarcinoma in the descending colon.

Please schedule a follow-up appointment as soon as possible to discuss these findings in greater detail, review the potential treatment options, and answer any questions you may have. We will also involve a surgical oncologist in your care, and we can facilitate that introduction.

Please know that we are committed to working with you to develop a personalized care plan that aligns with your needs and preferences. We can also connect you with resources for emotional and practical support to individuals facing colon cancer..."

This is an unexpected turn of events. Never could I have imagined I would uncover something like this. Considering how it was buried under piles of papers and the sealed envelope, I am wondering if Tom's family even knows. There has never been a single mention of him seeing a gastroenterologist or even a proctologist. Could it be that he didn't want to worry anyone? I need to read through these documents carefully in the privacy of my own home. Hopefully, then, I will get some additional details. Like what stage was it discovered, and did they give him a life expectancy timeline?

But for now, I could be on borrowed time. Helen only mentioned this trip to Cape May in passing. I didn't get many details. For all I know, they could be back at any time now.

I certainly don't want to get caught snooping if she suddenly comes home while I'm still here.

CHAPTER 25

KRISTY

The next twenty-four hours are very much like the first twenty-four. Amazing. And Leo taking the day off work tomorrow makes it even nicer. We all go walking through town, admiring the Victorian houses, aglow in warm white Christmas lights.

Glad Mom thought to pack the stroller—this would be way too much walking for Cozette's little legs to keep up. The monotonous bumping of the stroller puts her right to sleep for a nap and allows us to pull up chairs at the outdoor Winter Wonderland at a beautiful hotel called Congress Hall, another spot full of memories for Mom with Dad. Leo excuses himself to get in line for cocktails as Mom goes on and on about the history of the hotel, built in 1816.

I can't help but think that Mom is acting a bit distracted, like she's happy to be here and enjoying her time reminiscing, but her mind, at times, is elsewhere.

She looks out toward the ocean as she relives how she and my dad couldn't afford to stay here. "It was just as well; we got to walk through it and enjoy the amenities while still staying at The Beacon thirty-five years ago. And really, not much has changed, except for the clientele. Everyone seems so young!"

"Mom, maybe we're just getting older?" I cringe at the thought.

Leo returns with our three drinks, which probably cost as much as a room did thirty-five years ago. Yum, a caramel apple martini for me, an apricot sour for Mom, and Tito's and club for himself.

"The bartender had to ask three other bartenders how to make an apricot sour. Must not be a big seller," he says as he winks at Mom.

Leo can do no wrong in front of Mom. She just seems to like him more and more each day.

Mom hears a beep in her purse. Loudest notifications ever. When Mom's phone rings or has a message, I always look around as if to apologize to everyone around us. But no one here seems to notice. "Oh, that's nice. Marty is stopping over to put food in my refrigerator for when I return home."

"That is really nice. How has Marty been?" I ask.

"Umm, well, sadly, he's not doing well. Not only was Dad his best friend, but something tells me Dad was Marty's *only* friend. He couldn't keep himself together at Dad's funeral. The whole day probably brought back so much sadness just thinking about his own wife's funeral a couple of years ago. He's been bringing over food, which is nice, but I can't possibly eat it all. He just fills my fridge every other day. He wants to make sure I'm eating nutritious meals and not just snacks, I suppose."

"It's nice that cooking for you is giving him something to do, and I'm sure it makes him feel useful. I'd be happy to take some of that food off your hands," I offer.

As we're finishing up our drinks, Cozette starts to stir in her stroller. The Christmas lights and squealing kids wake her up faster than usual.

"Mommy, can I ride a horsey?" she asks, pointing to the merry-go-round.

"Okay, one ride on the horsey and then we'll walk to dinner." Although it's chilly, the weather has been more than cooperative. Nice enough to walk all day and evening with plenty of layers on.

Leo gets her out of her stroller, and she hits the ground running. I run after her and purchase tickets for the ride. The line moves quickly, and we get on the merry-go-round and do a full loop until she finds the perfect horse.

Purple mane and pink horse.

Smiling ear to ear, she is having the time of her life. What a thrill a merry-go-round is for little ones. When the ride comes to an end, it is quickly followed by "Again, Mommy!"

I would've been shocked if it ended any other way.

"No sweetie, one ride, then dinner, remember?" Much to her disappointment, we head back to our chairs, where Mom and Leo are waiting.

We let Mom pick the restaurant as we gather our things to head out. She wants to try a place called Fins, which is new since her last visit to Cape May. Apparently, she has done her research and tells us the restaurant is adorned with fish tanks to keep Cozette busy while we wait to be seated.

We have been out and about all day, and we all seem to be dragging. After dinner, I suggest we head back to The Beacon and watch Christmas movies.

Fortunately, we all agree.

Cozette has plenty of favorite shows, each one more high-def and brightly colored than the last. But when it comes to Christmas movies, I'm a sucker for the oldies. If it was made any time after 1980, I'm not interested.

Luckily for me, all Cozette knows as far as Christmas movies are concerned are *Frosty the Snowman*, *The Year Without a Santa Claus*, and *Rudolph*.

When we get back and into our jammies, I turn on the TV to catch *The Year Without a Santa Claus* halfway through. Heat Miser appears, mid-song. Oh, what great memories!

Snuggled up in blankets on the couch with Mom and the new Fudge, Cozette points to a picture on the wall. "Grams, what does that say?"

Mom puts on her reading glasses and says, "Would you believe, Cozy, I remember that picture! It says, *'If this isn't Heaven, what is?'*"

101

"What does that mean, Grams?"

"Well, it means this place is so perfect, how can Heaven be any better?"

"Oh," Cozette says, looking confused but also disinterested, as Snow Miser appears on the TV, and she is mesmerized.

I turn to face Leo. "Is it weird that I just got the chills when Mom read the quote on that picture?"

"Why would that give you chills?" He looked at me, confused.

"I have no idea. I've heard that phrase before. I mean, I'm sure everyone has at one point or another, but I feel like I heard it a lot. I just can't remember when or where."

As I snuggle back into Leo's shoulder, with his arm around me, I can't help but wonder how that saying means something to me and why.

CHAPTER 26

If this isn't Heaven, what is . . .

Well, The Beacon in Cape May certainly was. But that is not where I've heard the saying.

I thought about it for the rest of the evening and while lying in bed. But I can't say it kept me up, as I fell asleep about ten seconds after my head hit the pillow.

Walking all day in the fresh air while sightseeing is exactly what we needed. I feel refreshed and ready to start my week.

Heading home after the Mad Badder breakfast that I promised Mom is bittersweet. "I tell you, Kristy, the eggs Benedict this morning was very good, but I still think yours yesterday was the best I've ever had."

A good critique of eggs Benedict is one of the highest compliments that Mom can give. I'll take it.

"Well, thanks, Mom! I'm glad you enjoyed your weekend! We will have to make a point of doing this before Christmas every year."

"I'd love to. And next time, remind me to get saltwater taffy for my neighbor. She got my mail while we were away. I feel horrible showing up empty-handed when I go to pick up my mail," Mom says, looking disappointed in herself.

"Mom, we were gone only one mail delivery day. How much could you have possibly gotten?" I question.

"Who even gets mail? Don't you pay your bills online?" Leo takes a jab at her old-fashioned ways. She still writes checks every opportunity she gets and gets mad when they aren't accepted. And don't even get me started on Apple Pay.

Mom chooses to ignore him.

We aren't in the car for half an hour, and Cozette is already asleep, cuddling with her new Fudge.

"Mom, I know I've heard that saying on the picture from last night. But I can't think of where? Would you have any idea?" I ask, clearly running low on options.

"No, sweetie, I'm not sure. I mean, Dad said it often, but I don't know specifically where you would've heard him say it."

Interesting. That picture was there all those years ago; maybe that was intentional.

We arrive at Mom's house, and I help her with her bag as she unlocks the door and then grabs her mail from the neighbor. When I put her bag down upstairs in her room, I can't help but notice Dad's office door is open. That's strange.

I make a point of closing that door every time I leave his office after cleaning up the paperwork. It carries such a strong scent of Dad; I don't want Mom to be sad when she passes it in the morning. Why would it be open? Mom said being in there was too hard for her after she went in to collect a couple of trinkets and pictures from his desk.

I head downstairs with the intention of asking her who's been in Dad's office. When I round the corner at the bottom of the steps, I see her sitting at the kitchen table crying.

"Mom, what happened?"

"Oh, nothing happened. I just don't see a time when I will get my mail and not have something in there for Dad. Sometimes it's really hard to grasp that I'll never see him again."

I see Mom clutching the electric bill in her hand. One of the many bills that will have to be changed over into her name. This just sucks. Nothing I can say will comfort her this time.

"Hey, do you want me to have Leo take Cozette home, and I'll stay here with you?"

"Thanks, honey. But Sandra told me to call her when we got home; she wants to stop over. Maybe she'll stay the night with me."

"Okay, well, if she doesn't, and you want me to come back, I'm just a phone call away."

"Thank you, sweetie. You've done so much already. Go home with Leo and Cozette and have a nice night with them. I'll be fine."

I head back to the car, feeling guilty for not staying but also disappointed that I couldn't talk to Mom about the office door. I think that would've made her feel worse, not better.

As soon as I get in the car, I text Sandra. *"Hey, it's me. Can you pack an overnight bag when you go to visit Mom? I think she needs some company tonight. She won't ask, but she'd be thrilled if you stayed over. I don't think she wants to be alone right now."*

Sandra answers in a true Leo-like way, *"K."*

Does that mean, "K, I'll pack a bag and stay over," or "K, thanks for the heads up, I have no intention of staying over"?

This is yet another time that I wish I weren't such a control freak. I want to go home, order a pizza, put on my PJs and slippers, and veg. But it looks like instead I'm on call in case Mom needs late-night company.

CHAPTER 27

We finish up our pizza, and Cozette runs off to grab Fudge and watch her favorite cartoon.

As Leo and I are cleaning up the table, he looks at me and says, "It seems like you're extremely happy to be engaged, which makes me think you've already planned the wedding?"

"Oh, heck no! I am in no way ready at this exact moment to get married! But I am so incredibly happy to be engaged to you!"

Leo puts down the dish towel and grabs me by the waist to pull me closer to him. "No way ready at this moment to get married? Should I be insulted? Or more importantly, worried?"

"Oh, pah-lease. You know you are the only person I ever want to be with and will *always* ever want to be with. But doesn't our life seem pretty busy and complex at the moment? I am fine with being engaged for a bit before making it official. But it is the most amazing feeling being engaged to you.

"I have always known that you are mine, but this takes it to a whole new level. It's really, really sexy to be honest. I picture you wearing a ring that tells the world, 'Hey, I'm taken by this girl right here!' Nothing is hotter than that. Am I right?"

"Yeah, sure. But if we're being honest, I feel married to you already. Making it official is really for you, Cozette, and your family," he admits.

It's at that moment that my phone rings. I wonder why Mom is calling already; we just saw her not too long ago. "Hey Mom, what's up?" Admittedly, I answered without even looking at the screen on my phone.

"Hi, sweetie, I spoke with Sandra just now. Seems she has a last-minute date tonight and can't stop by until tomorrow. Any chance you don't have plans tonight?"

I assumed this would happen. A huge part of living footloose and fancy-free is being a wee bit irresponsible. I don't blame her, but yet again, I'm here to pick up the pieces.

"Sure, Mom, I can come back over! We just finished dinner, and Cozette is watching TV. Give me about a half hour."

I mouth to Leo, "*Sorry!*"

"It's fine. I should do some work before bed anyway. I have my computer here, so I'll stay over instead of heading home." Leo saves me every time. "And *Peppa Pig* is one of my favorites, so we're all good."

"Okay then, I'll give Cozette a kiss goodbye. Can you put her to bed before I get back?"

"Yup, and bring your mom the leftover pizza so I'm not tempted and finish it myself."

I kiss Cozette goodbye as she barely looks away from the pigs jumping in the muddy puddles, and I head off to Mom's with some pizza.

I get in my car by myself, which is a luxury. This is my favorite time of year for many reasons, but singing Christmas carols at the top of my lungs in the car is at the top of that list. Tuning into traditional Christmas classics never disappoints, and the singing begins.

Before I know it, I am pulling up to Mom's. Oddly enough, she is standing outside on her front stoop waiting for me.

"Hey! Why are you outside? It's getting really cold out here!"

"Oh, I wasn't feeling very comfortable inside alone, so I thought I'd come out here, get some fresh air, and wait for you," she admits.

Not comfortable inside alone? Mom might be one of the most independent people I know. And although I expected her to be devastated by losing her husband and best friend, it certainly wasn't because she was dependent on him.

"What do you mean, 'not comfortable inside'?"

"Come on in, I'll show you."

I follow Mom into the house. The scent of pine needles takes over as I walk in. It wraps around you like a big warm hug the very second you walk in the door.

She leads me to the kitchen as we pass through the dining room. The dining table is full of labeled Lenox serving pieces from what would have been our Thanksgiving dinner together.

Sadly, Thanksgiving came and went like it didn't even happen. The only reminder of the holiday was the wasted side dishes that I had to throw away the following week. What was once my absolute favorite holiday, within seconds, became the one I will now dread.

Mom walks into the kitchen and over to her junk drawer. She points to it as if speechless. I'm confused. "Kristy, someone was here, and they were rummaging through my drawers! I know it looks like a drawer full of junk to you, but it was very well-organized junk. I knew exactly where everything was in this drawer. I was in here getting a Band-Aid right before you picked me up for Cape May on Friday."

"Hmm, that *is* strange. Well, maybe Joe or Sandra stopped by for something? Did you ask them? Or how about Marty? He dropped off food for you, right?"

"No, I haven't. You're right, it probably was Sandra or Joe. Or maybe Marty. But I wonder what they would be looking for, especially in my junk drawer. I'll text them now. In the meantime, how about a cupatea?"

Now that she's got me here until I at least finish my mug, she knows I won't be running out the door.

I remind her to text my siblings as she's looking for the honey, no doubt a little package taken from the local diner. Leo will tease Mom whenever we go out to eat. If the jelly and sweeteners aren't nailed down to the table, they are going in her purse. "They are on the table *for us*; it's not stealing. I *will* use this jelly, just not right now," is her justification every time.

"Yes, yes, thank you. It's been difficult lately to multitask. Here you go. Here's the honey, and the water will be ready in a minute. I'll text them now."

Within minutes, her phone beeps obnoxiously. Both Sandra and Joe answer quickly with disappointing responses. Neither says they were here over the weekend, and Sandra questions why. Joe just answers *"no."*

Seconds later, Marty replies, *"Nope. I was in your house only for the minute it took to put your dinner in the fridge. Sorry I can't be more helpful."*

That is very unsettling.

I know Mom has been forgetting things; maybe she rummaged through it herself. Maybe not. Either way, I'm glad I'm here. I had better text Leo to tell him that I'm staying the night.

I understand why she felt uncomfortable being in the house alone. I'm starting to feel uncomfortable in this house, too, and I'm not even alone.

I am most definitely having Mom change her locks. Better yet, I'm just going to do it myself—tomorrow.

I'll give her the new keys, and she won't be able to object because it will already be done.

CHAPTER 28

I wake up bright and early to the sound of Mom's grandfather clock chiming every hour on the hour. Truth be told, I *woke up* every hour on the hour due to the clock. Zero REM.

For whatever reason, I am wired even with the lack of sleep. Knowing I must hit the ground running today makes me spring out of bed.

I left a Post-it note for Mom. I don't want to wake her, but I really can't linger. I head to my apartment and let myself in to the glorious smell of coffee. Leo is as quiet as a mouse, and Cozette must be sleeping because I can hear a pin drop in here. Literally. Drop a pin, and it would clang for all to hear.

As I turn the corner, looking for any signs of life, I see Leo exiting the bathroom. "Impeccable timing!" I say to Leo as he stands there in a towel. Wow, his morning workouts have really chiseled his chest and arms; it looks like they are made of stone. The very last thing I want to think of right now is getting Cozette ready for preschool. But sadly, we're behind schedule as is, and I need to get her up.

I can count on just one hand the number of times I've said that. I'm guessing Leo had her up later than she's used to. But I don't bother asking, as I don't want anything to interrupt his sensual kissing.

"Mommy home!" Well, there it is. Inevitable, yes. But bad timing, also yes.

"Good morning, sweetie! Give me a big hug, and then go brush your teeth. I'll make your eggs, and we'll get moving to school!"

"OK, Mommy, but Fudge is sick, so I think I'll stay home with her."

Oh, heck no. Mommy has too much to do today. Starting with Leo. And then, of course, working the lunch shift, then changing Mom's locks, and all the while, trying to figure out Dad's riddle. Did he have more to say? Is his quest just to force me to take a walk down memory lane and appreciate all that I have? And most importantly, to appreciate the journey itself? Because, like he wrote, *"Live in the moment, and enjoy your life... don't forget to look around and enjoy the sights from time to time..."*

That is exactly what I've been doing. When Cozette asks me a question, she has my full attention. When Leo and I are intimate, he gets all of me, my mind completely focused on him. And I've been much more patient with Mom. Even drinking tea again.

I begrudgingly leave Leo in a towel to talk to Cozette about how she is, in fact, going to school.

"Hey, sweetie, I'm sorry Fudge isn't feeling well, but you can take care of her at school today. I'm sure all she needs is rest, so you'll be able to put her down for a nap at school while I'm at work, okay?" She seems to like the idea of taking care of her dependent in front of her friends, so my suggestion went over much better than I anticipated.

As I go into the kitchen, I peek my head into my bedroom. "If you're not in a hurry, stay here a bit, and I'll come right home from drop-off!" I guess that's all he needed to hear because within minutes, I hear him typing away on his computer.

After eggs are made and the kitchen is cleaned up, I change Cozette, do her hair, throw on her coat, and out the door we go.

Drop-off is back to normal since the new Fudge entered our lives. She happily jumps out of the car after being unbuckled and runs up the pathway to Ms. Lauren. There is a special place in my heart for Cozette's favorite teacher, Ms. Lauren. She greets the children each day, looking like a cross between Cinderella and Sleeping Beauty, with her flowing hair, flawless skin, and glistening smile. The kids almost instantaneously fall in love with her warm, welcoming voice and demeanor.

As I'm driving home, I get a very weird sensation, like tingles under my skin. What on earth could be causing this? I drive this exact route at least twice a day and have never had this feeling. My subconscious seems to be acting on its own.

Driving along the park, the tingles become almost unbearable. The repressed part of my brain is trying to tell me something; I just need to catch up.

I pull over to the side of the road at a very familiar spot. Dad and I used to sit on this special bench and talk about the historic home that was demolished exactly where we were in 1970.

We always tried to envision living like they did in 1713, in that house, with no electricity or running water, having to go to the well to retrieve water, and not having a candy store in town. Of course, that was always where my mind went.

I get out of the car and meander over to the bench, fearing that if I sprint, people will be concerned.

Dad absolutely loved our time here together. At least he seemed to. He was always smiling and positive. Sitting on that bench was the highlight of both of our days.

What was it that Dad would say each time we had to get off this bench to go home for dinner?

"If this isn't Heaven, what is?"

CHAPTER 29

I have to say I didn't see this coming.

Dad was always such an inspiring man, and I truly was beginning to think he wanted me to stop and smell the fictitious roses.

And yet here we are. The picture at The Beacon, which Mom remembered, *was* significant.

It has been decades since Dad and I sat on that bench and daydreamed. I find myself daydreaming now as I sit on it, just like I used to. Noticing the beautiful shrubs that have since been planted and how well-kept the grounds look. Quite possibly just as nice back then, but my attention to detail would have been more focused on a ladybug on the bench than the landscape.

It's not surprising that it didn't come to me right away when I saw the picture in Cape May. Sometimes it takes a special place or a certain smell to spark your memory. Then you're shocked you didn't think of it sooner. I'm just glad it finally hit me. If this clue and what Dad has to say next went undiscovered, I would be heartbroken.

I sit here taking it all in for quite a while.

How they connect, and what comes next, could be challenging to solve. I have to tell Leo and lean on him for help. *Leo*!! He is waiting at my apartment for me! I can't believe it slipped my mind. This has preoccupied me to the point of complete tunnel vision. I hadn't thought of Leo since I left to drop off Cozette. It must have been at least an hour since I've been gone. Why did I leave my phone in the car?

I am never without it. He's probably been calling to see if I'm okay!

I race back to my car to see no missed calls, but one text. *"I couldn't wait any longer. I'll call you tonight after work."* Shit! Shit! Shit!

I was so looking forward to coming home to him and spending quality alone time together. Ugh. Guess now I'll have more time to shower and get ready for work. Plus, I can focus on Dad's latest quest.

I think I'll accomplish more if I am actually *on* the bench. Look at what one visit did. I took Dad's game to the next level by just immersing myself in the moment.

I need to focus. Shower. Work. Pick up Cozette. Make dinner. There is not much wiggle room there. And it gets dark by 4:30 now, so after dinner won't be an option. Do I call out of work for this? It is one hundred percent what I want to do. But my bank account one hundred percent wants me to go to work.

The responsible choice wins again. This will have to wait. Maybe I'll grab something for dinner for Cozette and Mom and ask her to come over to visit with Cozette for a bit. I can run out quickly and see if there is anything obvious for me to uncover. If not, at least I tried, and I can get back at it over the weekend, when my mornings aren't as chaotic.

I am feeling a bit guilty for keeping this to myself, though. Sandra, Joe, and especially Mom should know about Dad's messages to me. I would be pissed if they kept these little Dad nuggets to themselves.

Finally, I have a plan. Invite Mom over for dinner and tell her why I need to quickly step out. Of course, I have to consider the excruciatingly long explanation I'll have to give. But for now, I'm just discussing this with Mom. I won't be able to handle Sandra's incessant questioning and Joe's utter lack of interest.

Chickie's and Pete's will get to see their most undependable employee earlier than expected, which never happens. Who in the food and beverage industry would show up to work early? My intention is to be the first to go home if we are slower than usual. That's all I can hope for. But with the Christmas season upon us, I'm guessing there will be a line outside the door.

I pull into the parking lot, and as expected, it's packed already. I text Mom and ask her to come over for dinner when I'm done working. She's never said no when I've extended a dinner invitation. It must be something within that generation. Do not waste so much as a morsel of food, and do not ever, ever, say no to your daughter's dinner invitation.

I'm sure it's because Mom put so much pressure on herself to provide perfect meals every single night for my dad as soon as he returned from a day at work.

A protein, a vegetable, and a starch, as she would call it, all must be present every night. Man, that *is* pressure. Our generation is so different. If I don't feel like cooking, I don't. I would order DoorDash, which Mom wholeheartedly does not believe in. "By the time you pay the fees and delivery, not to mention the tip, you've doubled the cost of your meal!" she will say at any mention of DoorDash.

And if not delivered, then I'll just ask Leo to cook. Guys these days are prepared to share all roles and responsibilities, in and out of the house. Not one day in my life have I ever felt pressure in the kitchen.

As far as Mom's thought process about dinner, it's not exactly the same as mine. Dinner is just something she gets out of the way so that she can have dessert. It's fascinating to see her pick at her food and eat like a bird, just so she can say, "I ate my dinner. Now I can have my dessert." It's like she's six years old, and her mom is looking over her shoulder. I'm not sure who she is hoping to get approval from.

If it's me she is expecting to hear positive recognition from because of her diligent dinner accountability, she's mistaken. I would be the first person to applaud if she had a bowl of chocolate ice cream with wet walnuts smothered on top. But eww, wet walnuts. Mom has never had ice cream without them.

As I am walking through the door to my loud, energetic place of employment, my phone dings. It's the wet walnut lover, herself.

"Sorry, honey, I can't come over to your house for dinner tonight. Marty is coming here for dinner."

CHAPTER 30

Well, that was certainly not expected. Marty? For dinner? Dropping off dinner, yes. Staying for dinner, though? I guess it'll be good for them to be able to swap Dad stories. She has spent every day since Dad's funeral with her kids and granddaughter. Adult conversations may be good for her.

There goes my well-thought-out plan. I've waited this long; what's another day?

Now that I am not rushing to get home, I should probably take advantage of this merry crowd and work as late as I can. I text Leo to let him know we're going to stick to the plan of him picking up Cozette, but not to expect me any earlier than usual.

I manage to break away from the floor just long enough to call Mom to see what's happening at home. It rings and rings, but puts me into voicemail. Voicemail? Have I ever even gotten Mom's voicemail? She usually answers before the second ring.

Okay, well, I have to get back to my tables, so checking on Mom again will have to wait. Being so busy does make the time fly. But every free second I have, I am pondering Dad's message. This is more than a coincidence.

If this isn't Heaven, what is?

First thing tomorrow, before Leo heads out the door, I am going to that bench. I need to see what comes to me, if anything.

A couple of hours later, when the crowds seem to die down a little, Mom texts. *"Hi sweetie! I'm hoping everything is OK?! I don't think you have ever called me from work. Anyway, my ringer was off, which is weird because I don't even know how to turn it off. Not sure how that happened. I'm calling back to see if everything is fine. OK, call me when you can. I love you!"*

Ringer off? This from the woman who tried to convince me that her phone did *not* have a shut-off feature. That is really strange. I must add "Ask Mom about her memory, blood work, and doctors' appointments" to my to-do list for tomorrow.

But until then, table number 12 needs more ketchup.

After my shift, I walk into my apartment to my two favorite people lying on the couch in front of the TV, sound asleep. I can't wait for the day when this is the norm and the three of us officially live together.

When I have a more rewarding nine-to-five job, then I'll have it all.

But as my dad would say, "Live in the moment and enjoy your life. You only get one."

He is right. He was always right. I go to the fridge, grab a bottle of wine, and pour myself a glass.

Maybe this is what he meant. I sit and enjoy my wine while my feet throb and my ears ring. I slip off my shoes and live in this moment for as long as I can. Before I wake them for bed, I just enjoy the calm. I cherish the peace. Life will always be hectic. It will always be overscheduled and chaotic. These are the sweet spots. The times we'll look back on and say, "Remember when Cozette was little enough to snuggle up with us on the couch and fall asleep in our arms?"

I don't appreciate times like this as much as I certainly should. Well, I am definitely appreciating this one.

Until my phone beeps. A text from Mom. *"Hi honey, I haven't heard back from you, so I'm guessing you and Cozette are fine. OK, I'm heading up to bed. Call me tomorrow!"*

I cannot forget to ask her about her dinner tonight. I get that Marty is lonely without Dad around, but I really hope he doesn't make a habit of this. I'm sure he does find comfort in having a peer to reminisce about their deceased spouses. I need to try to be more patient with him.

Cozette snuggles deeper into Leo's armpit. Now is the time to move her, or I'll never do it.

That relaxing moment was short-lived, but at least now I'll get to fill in the empty spot that Cozette will leave and snuggle with my fiancé.

My fiancé. Oh, how I love the sound of that.

CHAPTER 31

In staying true to my word, I am the first one up. Leo never sleeps past 6:00, unless it's Saturday. And only then, I may occasionally catch him in bed until as late as 7:30.

Now is one of those rare moments, 6:45, and he's still sound asleep. I guess my keeping him up half the night could be to blame, or to thank, as it turns out. But I am too excited to sleep any longer. As my coffee is brewing, I write a quick note to Leo: *"Went to pick up bagels, be back soon!"*

We are out of bagels, and I actually *do* need to pick some up for our breakfast sandwiches this morning. John's Friendly Market has the freshest bagels around, and I pass right by it on the way to the park bench. It also has the most wholesome name ever. John's was my first job while I was in high school. Just about every teen in town has worked at John's at some point before leaving for college and then again when coming back for summers. I love how that store has apparently not changed a bit in well over one hundred years.

I dart into John's Market, leaving my car running, barely checking for traffic as I race across the street. This must be quick. The sweet elderly ladies who work the registers will have to understand: no small talk today.

I grab an everything, a plain, and a sesame seed bagel and run out the door after throwing a five-dollar bill on the counter. "Thanks! See you tomorrow!" I say to them. I don't have the heart to ignore them completely, even in my big rush.

Okay, here it goes! Back to the bench to maybe find some answers. I zip around the swerved road, circling the park. When I see it, I pull over to the side of the street, again throwing on my hazard lights.

Passing the lawn plaque, describing the home that once stood here and its significance to the town, I head right to the bench. Wait, is there some kind of clue on the sign? I turn back around and read it over and over again, but nothing pops out at me. Okay, I can come back to this if I need to. Let me just have a seat and envision my little girl self sitting with my dad.

It's a chilly December morning, but the trails are still full of people, even at 7 a.m. I watch the steam exit my warm mouth and wonder who would *choose* to go outside for a run on a December morning.

Apparently, many people choose just that.

As I sit, I recite those meaningful words my dad would say every time we sat here.

"*If this isn't Heaven, what is?*"

"I don't know, Dad! I just don't know! I could really use some help right now. I know you have more to say to me, and I'd give anything to hear it. I just need a little guidance with this one!" I say while looking up to the sky.

As I sit here talking to myself, I look around for passersby who think I've lost it. Every single person has earbuds in, so for all they know, I'm just lip-syncing to my favorite song on my earbuds.

That's when I notice a little girl, no older than five or six, jumping down and climbing up the stone fence that still stands. I think back to Dad holding my hand as I attempted to walk the entire length of the long wall like a tightrope.

This was our routine. He would hold my hand and cheer me on the entire way, as if I were fifty feet in the air. His one hand in mine, and my other stretched as far out as it would go, like I would see them do in the circus.

Every time we'd come to a spot on the fence with a missing stone, Dad would say, "Lava!" and I'd jump over the vacant hole. The fence is hundreds of years old, so there were quite a few missing stones along the way.

I get up from the bench to get a closer look at the ancient wall of stone. As I approach, the little girl runs off to her mom, standing on the trail with a stroller carrying a younger sibling, as they patiently wait for her.

The wall looks exactly the same as I remember it. I suppose twenty-five years is nothing when it's been standing for hundreds. I attempt to walk across, like I did as a child, holding my dad's hand.

Now I don't even care who's watching. This is bringing me right back to my childhood. Along with smells and sounds, feelings can also bring you back to a moment in time.

I need to bring Cozette here and see if she enjoys this park as much as I used to. I continue to jump the bits of lava, like I did as a kid. I can almost hear Dad exclaim, "Lava!" with each missing rock.

When I finally get to the end, I jump down and walk around to the front of the wall. This would have been where the front of the house stood. It must have been magnificent when it was still standing.

The hide-and-seek games that Dad would play with me down here were probably my favorite part of our excursion. We would act like Sherlock Holmes and look for anything out of the ordinary. At the time, I thought it was magical how we could practically wish something into existence. When it was just Dad leading the way but making me think they were my ideas.

"Kristy, do you think something is hiding in that big patch of new grass?" Or "If somebody wanted to hide something valuable, they could probably do it in those big, intertwined tree roots..." he would say.

Inevitably, we would run over to the spot, and I would search. Sometimes he even thought of bringing a magnifying glass. Not that it even worked, but I didn't know the difference. All I knew was that it made me feel very official.

And with each new discovery, something *would* be hiding in the crevice. A nickel, or a Tootsie Roll, and once a treasure map for him and me to follow.

Wow, I can't remember the last time I thought about those special moments. All the work and effort he would put into those magical days for me. And that's exactly what I thought they were: magic. Little did I know Dad would drive down to the park and plant the goodies before we went for our walks that always ended at our bench destination.

For an adventurous kid like me, this really *was* Heaven.

I don't recall where the treasure map took us. But I am sure he would let me lead the way, and he would just act like my sidekick. I do remember what the paper map smelled like. It was the distinct, strong smell like when Mom would blow out candles after a party. A kind of burnt wax and smoky scent. I loved that smell. It only smelled like that after a special occasion, a party, or church.

Dad informed me it must have been from the cardstock's burnt edges, like an old pirate's treasure map where X marked the spot. I definitely can recall how I found the treasure map.

"Kristy, if we can find a loose rock in this wall, I'd be willing to bet there's a treasure behind it," he would say, obviously having planted the surprise earlier that day.

How crazy would I look if I started pulling at these rocks to find a loose stone right now? Crazy or not, I'm doing it. I start at the very beginning—this could take a while. I tell myself if I don't find whatever I'm looking for by the time I reach the stone steps, the halfway point, I'll head home. I could then go home, make breakfast, and maybe bring Cozette back later today.

To my surprise, there are several loose stones that give way to my insistent pulling and break free. None of which hides anything but bugs and spiderwebs. I keep going, hoping for something, anything, to help me figure out what I am supposed to do next.

I am nearing the stone steps and ultimately the end of my morning in the park.

Until I come across a rock that looks a bit different from the rest. It's a perfect fit in the wall, of course, but there's something off about it. The moss that surrounds every other rock has been compromised on this one, like someone has been poking around more recently than hundreds of years ago.

I give it a good jiggle, and it easily comes out, falling into my hands.

This crevice holds more than just spiderwebs. I see an object, but I can't make it out. I retrieve my phone and shine the flashlight toward the back of the deep opening.

What on earth could this be? My hands are shaking as I reach into the crevice. Oh my gosh, it can't be. My dad was here. My dad left me a message. And he has more to say to me.

CHAPTER 32

I hustle to get back to my apartment. It's after eight, so I can only hope that Leo woke up later than 7:30 and thinks he just missed me before I left. Or else, no doubt he's worried. I fumble with my keys and quietly let myself in. As expected, they are on the couch watching *Peppa Pig*. I hold up the bagels and announce, "Bacon, egg, and cheese sandwiches coming right up!"

Leo looks over at me. Slowly, he gets up. Cozette is so fixated on the TV that she doesn't even notice that Leo's moved, which I'm guessing is what he was hoping for. "Where did you rush off to so early this morning?"

"I'm sorry, I tried not to wake you."

"Yes, but you did, and you're not answering my question," Leo says with a straight face, which tells me he is running out of patience.

With Cozette giggling in the background, I start taking the bagels out of the bag and explain my absence.

"Right, okay, so I've been giving my dad's letters and clues a lot of thought. Like, a lot. I can't stop thinking about them. In the middle of the night, I sit up when I think I've figured something out. Last night I remembered where I've heard, 'If this isn't Heaven, what is?'" I say as I'm slicing bagels and placing them in the toaster oven.

"I just had to go there first thing this morning. Oh yeah, and get bagels."

"Well? Are you going to keep me hanging? Where *is* this second heaven?" Leo asks as he blows on his coffee. I make myself a giant cup as I explain the park bench.

He seems completely intrigued, and I haven't even gotten to the good part yet.

"So, as I get to the unique rock and it comes loose in my hands, I see that this one is different; this is it. This is most certainly a message from my dad." I gulp my coffee.

"This is all so incredible. He is tapping into parts of your brain that had to be dusted off and brought back to the present. What a gift. What did you find? Where is all of this leading?" he asks, all while still blowing on his coffee, and I am finishing my huge mug.

"Yes, it is incredible. This is what I found behind the rock."

I uncurl my fingers to reveal a miniature statuette of an eagle. No bigger than a figurine from Monopoly.

"What is this?" Leo questions.

"It's a miniature bronze eagle."

"Yes, that I can see. But what is the significance?"

"It's quite significant. My parents would take the three of us to John Wanamaker's in Philadelphia every year around Christmas. They put on a wonderful holiday light show around the clock in December. We loved that trip so much. The whole family would take the Speedline train over to Philadelphia from Haddonfield, we'd go to the show, and then stop at the Gallery Mall for lunch. That day, every year, just screams "Christmas" for my family. It's when we officially start getting in the Christmas spirit. And the bronze eagle was at the center of it all."

Leo, still looking confused, says, "Okay, you had me until the eagle being at the center of it all. What does an eagle have to do with Christmas?"

"Wanamaker's was an enormous department store many years ago.

The grand lobby had a cathedral ceiling that spanned eight floors. And the eagle was right in the center of the lobby. 'If anyone ever gets lost, just meet at the eagle,' Dad would remind us every single year."

"I had forgotten all about this souvenir that he bought for us. I'm sure Joe lost his on the Speedline home, and I have no idea where Sandra's ended up. But I kept mine in my desk drawer with my scented erasers and markers. Ya know, all my important valuables."

I hear, "Mommy, can I have some eggs!?" coming from the couch.

If our recent meals are any indication of the menu in my future restaurant, I'll only be serving eggs.

Heading to the fridge for a carton of eggs, I finish my theory. "So, he probably wants us to go to the city and see the light show! Every year, I say that I'm taking Cozette to see the show, but it has never happened. We get busy, life gets in the way, and we never do fun adventures like my parents did with us. I need to get better at that.

All my most memorable moments from childhood come from doing things like that. My best times are adventures, not things. I need to keep reminding myself that that is what's most important!"

"Okay, so let's go tomorrow. I have a couple of meetings today, but nothing at all tomorrow, which is perfect timing too. We haven't given much thought to Christmas this year with everything going on. Let's take Cozette to the light show and stop for lunch like you did when you were little. I think that will put all of us in the Christmas spirit," Leo declares.

He's right. We haven't given Christmas much thought. Our lives have been crazy since Thanksgiving Eve, which feels like yesterday, not weeks ago. I can't even bear to think of my mom waking up alone on Christmas morning.

Okay, that settles it. Tomorrow morning we'll head to the train station to go to Philadelphia. "She will love it."

"Cozette, tomorrow we're going on an adventure!"

CHAPTER 33

Fortunately, at this time of year, the trains run every twelve minutes. So, although we see one pulling away when we turn into the parking lot, we only wait minutes on the cold platform until the next one pulls up.

Cozette has only been on the train a handful of times, and probably when she was still in an infant carrier.

The past two holiday seasons, I have been focusing on working extra hours to try and put away as much money as possible, in the hopes of moving Cozette and me into a bigger place.

For Cozette, this will be a new and exciting experience. We wait at the very beginning of the platform to ensure a first car and possibly a first-row seat.

Come to think of it, Leo and I have never been on the train together either. Any time we go into the city, he insists on driving. Leo likes to have complete control of his Irish goodbye getaways. And pulling off a good Irish goodbye does not involve standing around waiting for a train. So, this is a first for us!

The train pulls up to our stop, and we let the passengers exit the train before shuffling in and grabbing a seat. Second row, yay! Cozette will get a good view from here, especially sitting high up on Leo's lap. We only live about ten minutes over the bridge from Philadelphia, but with the multiple stops, we should be there in about twenty minutes.

A couple of stops later, the teens in the front row exit the train. Without hesitating, we jump into the front. I remember sitting here whenever we could when we came over as a family. I would pretend to be the train conductor, and Sandra would keep her eyes focused straight ahead so as not to get motion sickness.

Cozette talked a mile a minute the entire way. Most of the conversation was her explaining to Fudge what we were doing on the train, where we were going, and not to be scared. She loves acting like a little Mommy.

Six stops and nineteen minutes later, we arrive at Market Street in Philadelphia. The only part of this trip that I really dislike is the intensely strong smell of urine that smacks you right in the face as the train doors open. Being underground is just gross, and we can't get up the stairs fast enough.

I just follow the sounds of the bell ringing Santas on the street, collecting money in their red hanging pails. Taking a nice big gulp of fresh air as we step outside, I grab Cozette's mittened hand in mine, and Leo puts his leather-gloved hand in her other. My other hand holds tightly onto Fudge. I cannot risk losing her again!

Leading the way, I see that Wanamaker's is directly across the street from the train station.

We follow the sea of people crossing Market Street to window shop or possibly go to lunch or work. But wherever they're headed, everyone is in such a hurry this time of year.

I guess having only one child, who isn't even in grammar school yet, means my upcoming years are bound to become more and more hectic. It's not lost on me that being able to take a day before the holiday to come into Philly on a whim is quite special.

We hold tight to Cozette's hands, knowing that if we let go, she could easily get carried off with the tsunami of this crowd. It looks as though we may have just missed a light show, from the sheer number of people exiting the store.

We head right toward the bronze eagle, which is hard to miss, standing eight feet tall in the middle of the grand lobby. Leo is looking around at the mass of people gathered too close for his liking. Between the potential for pickpockets and the likelihood of germs in the crowd, not to mention Leo's slight bit of social anxiety, this is surely an overload.

Zero personal space here. I guess he didn't believe me when I said this was extremely popular with people far and wide. And it appears everyone has the same meeting place: the eagle.

The digital sign above says, *"Next show in 6 minutes."* Great, not too much longer for fidgeting Cozette to have to wait. And I'll get a few minutes to check out this statue and see if there's anything significant or meaningful in the general vicinity. There are children climbing all over it. Too tempting not to. Cozette sees kids climbing, so of course, she wants to be climbing, too. My parents would never let us do this. I'm wondering what Dad would say if he could see Cozette, arms around the bird's neck, smiling ear to ear. Maybe they didn't let us, fearing we'd rip our tights. Mom took every opportunity she could to dress us in our matching "Sunday best," as she would call it.

Poor Joe. I never considered how he felt about wearing red plaid pants to match our Christmas plaid dresses. Dorky at the time, but adorable pictures to look back on now.

At first glance, it is nothing but a big bird. Leo is scouring it, too, also having no idea what he's scouring for.

The statue is exactly the same as it was twenty-five years ago, but back then it seemed so much bigger. Before coming back today, I would've guessed this eagle was twenty feet tall. That's exactly how it probably appears to Cozette now.

Two minutes until showtime. Which, from beginning to end, may last eight to ten minutes tops. For the next two minutes, with one hand on Cozette, I feel around the bronze statue. I wish I had brought hand sanitizer. Parts of the statue are sticky and smell of cherry, as if lollipops were stuck to it at one point. How many hands have touched this statue today alone? And of those hands, how many were attached to germy, sick kids? I can't think about that now. That explains why Leo is simply using his eyes and not his hands to inspect the statue.

The lights dim; the show is about to begin. We choose to sit on the lobby floor, like everyone else, straining our necks to see all the way to the top of the enormous screen of lights.

It is exactly as I remember it, down to the narrator and music. Wow, this holds the fondest of memories. It's unbelievable how quickly they flood back. I can practically hear Sandra getting so excited at this part, with Rudy the Teddy Bear playing the drum. And me being amazed at the technology that allowed Frosty to dim slowly until he was gone, as if melting.

Such simple times. This really gives me perspective. Now I can just about guess what's going on in Cozette's little head. At the moment, she is mesmerized. I'm not sure she's blinking. I'm not sure Leo is either.

Growing up with all brothers, and many of them, Leo and his family didn't ever travel into the city like this. His mom would basically hold the front door wide open until each one went outside to play. From breakfast until dinner, those boys were outside riding bikes and getting into mischief. No cell phones and no idea as to where they were going and what they were getting into. I can't even imagine living in such a carefree world nowadays.

The show is just about over, and at this rate, we may be able to see it again. I haven't found anything noteworthy yet. It'll be easier to really inspect once the show is over and the kids are down. Where are their parents anyway?

It ends with a spectacular organist playing "Joy to the World," and just like that, the lights are back on.

Kids are hopping down off the statue's platform and running to whom I hope are their parents.

I place Cozette back on the eagle, just to have a little elbow room to look around. With her spread out on the bronze feathers, it's less likely to get covered with twenty-five other kids.

Standing with such authority in the middle of the giant store's lobby, this eagle has a majestic air about it. This powerful bird has a fearless demeanor with his keen gaze and sharp talons, looking like he's waiting to strike his prey.

Skimming my hand over the texture, I realize how intricate this statue is. Every one of the thousands of feathers looks as if it were individually placed in the perfect spot.

The spot where they would spend the next hundreds of years.

There is nothing I can see or feel on this statue whatsoever. Cozette is scootching higher and higher on the bird as she says to me, "Mommy, is the bird's name Fudge?"

"No, sweetie, just your doggie; this bird has a different name."

"What bird's name?"

"Hmm, that's a good question. He definitely has one. Or maybe Grams and Poppy named him for us. I can't remember what it was, but if I do remember, I'll tell you!"

"Grams will 'member!"

At this point, Leo is over the bird's name conversation and chimes in, "Yes, Grams will remember, but there's another crowd coming in, so we should think about heading out."

"Okay, we can go. Let me just get a picture of you two by the bird," I say, sounding defeated after finding nothing.

Hearing a train approach, we run down the subway steps. I remember to get my last big inhale before going underground. Leo is carrying Cozette and is a good six feet ahead of me. He jumps onto the train, then holds the door to ensure I get in before it closes.

Such a rush to catch a train after running for it. There is no better sigh in the world than the one exhaled as you sit in the train, after just making it.

"Cozette, did you like the show?" I ask.

"YES!" she squeals.

"What was your favorite part? I think mine is the Nutcracker, when he cracks the nuts."

"My favorite is the birdy," she exclaims.

Of course it is. This kid has such a soft spot for animals of all kinds.

When I took Cozette to the Philadelphia Zoo, we stood by every habitat as she asked question after question about each animal.

"When is giraffe's bedtime? What does lion eat for breakfast? Where is zebra's mommy?"

It's so cute to have a glimpse of what's going on in that little brain of hers.

"What birdy's name?"

Oh my god with the bird's name already.

"Do you want to call Grams and see if she remembers?"

"Yay!" she squeals.

I pull up Mom's number, hit call, and hand the phone to Cozette. Meanwhile, Leo and I can discuss dinner plans.

"Grams? What birdy's name?" I probably should've realized that Mom would have no idea what Cozette is talking about. I ask Cozette for the phone and explain to Mom that Cozette really wants to know what we called the eagle.

"Haha, how can you forget? My gosh, Cozy is so much like you when you were her age. You asked Dad the same question! Off the cuff, he came up with Durana, because the color of the feathers is a unique Durana bronze that gives it that golden hue. You even named your goldfish Durana after that eagle. Sadly, goldfish Durana didn't last very long!"

Mom is all but singing on the phone. I haven't heard her this happy in a long time. I don't care what the reason is; I'm just glad she is starting to turn a corner.

I'm beginning to think there is absolutely nothing wrong with Mom's memory. Well, not long-term, at least. My gosh, how did she remember all of that? Of course, it's kind of coming back to me now that she explained it in such detail, but I don't know if I could've come up with that on my own.

I explain to Cozette the bird's name and why. I think I lost her halfway through. I'm sure she was hoping for a name along the lines of Pinky or Tucker, or something easier to say than Durana.

Instead of responding, she just snuggles up more with Leo and Fudge as her eyelids get heavier and heavier.

CHAPTER 34

September 6, 1995

"Daddy! Can I get that fishy? That one, that one! She's not just orange like the other fishes, she has a yellow stripe on her!" I exclaimed in the middle of the street at the fall festival.

"Those fishes are prizes, sweetie; we can't buy them. You have to win them," my dad explained.

"Okay! Can we?" Winning a fish seemed like a guarantee. An exciting guarantee!

"Well, you can certainly try. But we have to meet Mom, your brother, and your sister by the library soon. They went to get soft pretzels, and they're probably going to be waiting for us. You can try only as many times as this one dollar will get you. Okay?"

"Yay! Okay, Daddy! I'm going to win that one, and I'm going to name her Durana!"

"Wait, what are you going to name it?" Dad questioned.

"Durana. Like the big bird from the light show," I said, looking at him, like "duh"!

Dad stood there laughing, watching me try to throw the ping pong balls into the fishbowl. And when I landed the last ball with a big splash, he lifted me up as I squealed.

"Daddy, I won her! We can take her home now!"

While walking back carrying my fish in a bag, heading to introduce her to the rest of the family, I asked Dad why he was laughing at me.

"Oh, sweetie! I wasn't laughing at you. I was laughing because I'm just so happy. You make me happy, and I love the name you picked for your fishy; it made me smile."

That made me feel better. Nothing can make me sad —I won a fish; this is the best day ever!

September 8, 1995

"Mommy, Daddy! Look at Durana! I've never seen her float before, but she's really good at it! It looks like she's napping."

And that just might be the shortest duration any person has ever had a pet.

After Mom and Dad looked at each other in horror, they weakly attempted to describe a thing called "fish heaven." I wasn't buying it. Durana is most definitely not happier in heaven. I fed her so much fish food; she loved it. I probably gave her twenty meals a day instead of two. She loved me; I was sure of it.

As Dad removes Durana and her bowl from the bay window, I ask Mom where we can bury the fish. "I know just the spot! Right under the maple tree, so when I'm climbing the tree, I can think of her." With that, the toilet flushes. Now I've lost Durana twice in one day. And the last time seemed extremely permanent.

"Dad, what are you doing? We're burying her outside!"

The second horrified look from Dad in minutes.

"Um, no, sweetie. That's not what happens when a fish dies. You flush the fish; you don't bury it. I'm sorry."

To console my tears over what is quickly becoming the worst day of my short life, Dad tells me he has a better idea. "Instead of burying the fish, let's write her letters and draw pictures of her and bury those."

With that, Joe walks into the kitchen, where I am staring at the empty bay window, and declares, "Kristy, you wouldn't bury a fish anyway; birds would eat it. If you want to keep her, you'd put her in the freezer." My little brother is so gross.

"That's enough, Joe. We would not put Durana in the freezer," Mom says, I'm sure just to reassure me that this was never an option.

So, picture drawing I did. My letter turned out to be more of a post-card. But it kept me occupied to the point that I forgot Dad had even disposed of her.

"Okay, Dad, I'm ready to bury these!" Joe looks at me and rolls his eyes. Joe always rolls his eyes at me. And Sandra is playing with her dolls quietly in the corner. Now seems like a good time to find a beach shovel and start digging.

Dad and I went out back to complete what seemed like a very normal task of burying drawings of a dead fish that I had for two days.

CHAPTER 35

MARTY

December 19, 2024

Ring, Ring, Ring...

"Hello?" Helen answers her phone on the last ring before voicemail.

"Grams, what's birdy's name?"

"Umm, what sweetie?"

"Oh, hi Kristy!... ha-ha, how can you forget?... Came up with Durana!.. Golden hue... goldfish... okay bye!"

Helen rolls back over onto me, her naked breasts on my bare chest.

"What the heck was that about?" I ask, extremely confused and a bit frustrated that our sex this evening was interrupted.

"The kids took Cozette to the light show in Philly, and she wanted to know the name of the big eagle in John Wanamaker's," Helen explains.

"Ya know what? I didn't understand a single word you just said, but I really couldn't care less about some eagle's name. So where were we?"

Instead of waiting for an answer, I kiss the nape of her neck, just the way she likes it.

CHAPTER 36

MARTY

When I sleep at Helen's, I always wake up when the sun rises. She loves the natural light coming into the bedroom, so the blinds are always halfway open. I, on the other hand, can't tell if it's day or night in my bedroom with my room-darkening shades.

I swing my legs out of bed and pull on my white T-shirt from last night.

"Before I head out this morning, let me help you with clearing out Tom's desk. I know it has been on your mind and that you've been procrastinating doing it. Let's just cross it off the list." I see a look of hesitation on Helen's face. "You will feel relieved when it's one less thing you have to do alone," I add, in the hopes she'll take me up on my offer.

"Oh, well, I really was not planning to do that today. I need to psych myself up for something like that, unfortunately."

"Nope. I insist! How about you get changed, and then we get started? I will go grab a box from my car."

I head out to my car to avoid hearing more protesting. I've taken the time to fill my backseat with all sizes of boxes, so if I am ever here visiting, I can kill two birds with one stone.

Maybe she'll just let me take care of this on my own. I would prefer not to have anyone breathing down my neck while I am going through his things anyway.

"I did tell Kristy that I would take care of the rest of Tom's office; she cleaned out the tedious filing cabinets. But there really is no hurry. You do not have to do this now, at 7:30 in the morning," Helen tells me, still trying to protest.

"I'm not going into the office until nine today, so this works out well," I answer.

"Okay, if you insist. I will go grab you some coffee then."

"That would be wonderful, thank you. I will get started on the desk while you're down there. Anything I should know about that you definitely want to keep?"

"At this point, no. If I needed it by now, I would have come in and gotten it, I suppose." Helen gives me permission to take everything, like I was hoping.

I will quickly grab a box and collect all the contents in and on the desk. That way, I can carefully go through all the items in the comfort of my own home.

Depending on how fast I can do this, I may even beat my coffee being brought up. That way, also avoiding any sentimental changes of heart to keep things. I do not have time for that. I really do need to get to work by nine.

My boss has been very lenient with my late arrival times at work this month. I guess that is what happens when your coworker and best friend dies unexpectedly.

Little do they know, I was just keeping my enemies closer.

CHAPTER 37

KRISTY

December 20, 2024

It is harder than usual to wake Cozette for preschool on this cold morning. Our trip into the city was more walking for her little legs and more stimulation than her normal day entails.

I try to coax her up out of bed twice before the shades roll up and my voice gets louder. In her defense, I didn't wake up this morning when Leo left either; I am just as tired. I let her stir for another moment as I get her outfit with hair bows out and ready to put on. "Up and at 'em, baby girl!"

I give her a big squeeze *good morning,* and then head into the kitchen to make her breakfast. I tend to do my best thinking while lying in bed at night, and last night was no exception. A combination of the peace and quiet, the dust settling from the day, and my physical exhaustion puts my mind in overdrive. Now my mind is consumed with my dad's messages and where they are ultimately leading me.

I'm going back to my mom's after I drop off Cozette. Now that Mom reminded me of my short stint as a pet owner, I remember burying something in the backyard by the maple tree. I could've saved us the trip to the light show had I remembered the eagle's name and therefore my fish's name. And therefore, most likely Dad's next "thing" for me!

But knowing Dad and what seems to be the point of this adventure, getting me over to the light show with Cozette was his plan. More memories remembered, and more memories made. *Thank you again, Dad.*

I am giddy as can be as I make breakfast in the kitchen. What could Dad have in store for me next? Will this fun adventure just go on and on? And when am I going to finally tell Mom and the siblings about this? I think it's well overdue, and now I'm starting to just feel sneaky.

I decide to go over to Mom's after dropping off Cozette and tell her before I go out back and dig. Maybe I will even suggest she join me in the digging. I'll let her know I asked her for dinner the other night so I could tell her this news, but she had plans with Marty. So it's not like I'm hiding it from her, I just don't think this is a conversation for a text message.

Cozette gets dressed, fed, teeth brushed, and out the door in record time. Nothing more motivating to get me moving than the chance to find something from Dad. If I am way off about this clue being buried, I will be super disappointed, as I have completely convinced myself that this is it.

Drop-off is done, and now I am heading to Mom's. Dropping Cozette at school has gone back to normal since the new Fudge. I love simple, drama-free drop-offs. I am hoping that revealing this information to Mom is equally uneventful, as I just want to get back to that maple.

Something tells me I should set aside a good amount of time to explain in detail what I've been up to this past week.

I can see from a block away that there is a different car in Mom's driveway. Who could be visiting her at 8:30 a.m.? It sure as heck won't be my brother or sister.

As I pull up to the house, I recognize the car. It's Marty's. Again. He is a nice guy and all, but I wish he'd just leave my mom alone and let her grieve in some peace.

I go right in and announce myself as I close the door behind me.

"Mom?" No answer.

"Mom!"

"Oh, hi, honey! We're upstairs!" *Upstairs? Why the hell are they upstairs?*

I take the steps two at a time and get upstairs short of breath. I can hear their voices in Dad's office.

"What are you doing in here?" I ask as I don't try to hide my disappointment and surprise.

"Oh, hi, Kristy! Your mom and I decided to tackle this desk today. One less thing for you to be burdened with!" Marty explains quite proudly.

"It's not a burden, Marty. I just haven't gotten to it yet. All the filing cabinets made my mind a bit numb, so I took a few days off. But you can go back downstairs; I'll finish in here. Mom, I was hoping to talk to you alone."

Marty and Mom exchange glances, and he announces he must get going anyway. He heads out with a box full of things.

Bye-bye, Marty! Don't let the door hit you in the ass!

"Mom, what was in the box Marty was carrying?"

"Just some junk that he said he would go through and throw out what he didn't want to keep. Some work papers, old lottery tickets, and stuff. Nothing exciting."

"Mom, could you please not give anything of Dad's away before asking us first?"

"Honey, you're being silly. It was all junk that I would've just thrown away anyway."

"I understand you think it was all junk. But I painstakingly went through each and every drawer of all of those filing cabinets, in case there was anything important in them. I would just appreciate the same courtesy when it comes to everything that belonged to Dad." I can't believe I need to explain this to my mother.

"Sure, sweetie. I will tell Marty that I don't need his help with anything else, and I'll just let you do it when you have the time. But his desk is cleaned out. I think the office is basically done."

How many times do I have to tell Mom, I WILL DO THIS! It is NOT a burden! This is the last of my dad's belongings, and I appreciate having the time and interest to go through it myself. Why does she insist on taking this away from me?

Now I just have to hope that there wasn't anything else special in there for me. Or anyone for that matter. Marty won't know what's junk and what's not. I am not happy. This is not how I expected the overdue conversation with Mom to start.

"Mom, I came here to talk to you about something. It's kinda important; if you wouldn't mind putting your phone down, so I can talk to you uninterrupted."

Again, I can't believe I need to explain this to my mother. And I can't help but notice how uncomfortable she looks at the moment.

"Sure, sweetie, what's up? This sounds serious...?"

"Well, it is serious, Mom. And I've been trying to find the right time to tell you."

Mom's eyes widen; she has no idea what I'm about to tell her.

"So last week when I spent some time in here, I found something."

Mom looks at me, discouraged, and says, "Please don't tell me there were unpaid bills in there."

"No, Mom, nothing like that. The only part of Dad's desk that I went through was the keyboard sliding drawer. It was my 'secret drawer' when I was younger. I wanted to check and see if my favorite stickers and erasers were still in there, but instead I found this."

I hand Mom the letter and let her read it herself.

Immediately, she reaches for the arm of his desk chair to lower herself into the seat, looking at me with a look I've never seen from her. Is it disbelief? Or anger that I didn't tell her sooner? It's best to sit quietly on the corner of Dad's desk until she's finished reading.

Moments later, she looks up again, speechless.

Finally, words escape her mouth: "We need to go to the old maple tree..."

This is where it's going to get tricky.

"Well, yes, but Mom, the thing is, I already went. And that's not all; there were more places to go. It's amazing! Dad has me traveling back in time to some of the most wonderful memories we made as kids."

I continue, as it seems she is unable to speak now.

"As it turns out, when I went to the tree, there was a carving in it. It just said *'Pic #1,'* which apparently meant the first picture we ever took in front of the maple. Leo and I looked through your albums in the basement and found it. It was from your birthday!"

"Wait. You're telling me that you've seen me and talked to me since you found this letter, and you haven't *told* me?"

"Fair enough. But at first I thought it was just the one stop, and I wanted to see what Dad wanted to share with me. I knew I would eventually tell you, but something in me wanted to keep it just between Dad and me for a bit. Then, when I realized he wasn't done, and there were more clues for me, I tried telling you. Well, I didn't get to *try, because* when I invited you over for dinner, Marty was coming over. And, by the way, he spends too much time here."

"Marty is irrelevant. What did you find when you located my birthday picture?"

"Here's the picture. He wrote on the back."

I pull the picture out of my back jeans pocket and hand it to her.

She scans the note quickly and then reads it again more slowly, her eyes tearing up as she reads,

"Starting with where your mom and I began our beautiful life together as husband and wife."

"Is this why the sudden, random trip to Cape May?" she rightfully asks.

"Yes. But better than just a random trip, there was another clue at The Beacon. You were helping all along, and you didn't even know it. The picture that you said was there when you visited thirty-five years ago was the answer. 'If this isn't Heaven, what is?' is a quote Dad would say to me every single time we sat on our bench in the park."

Mom is now listening intently.

"So, when we came back home, I went to the park. After some reminiscing and searching, I found this." Mom takes the little bronze eagle into her hands. It is no bigger than a quarter. She squeezes it, I'm guessing, because it's something Dad touched, and she hopes to feel his warmth.

"I forgot all about these little eagles that we bought for the three of you. Gosh, I haven't seen them in decades. This explains your trip with Cozette on Sunday to see the light show," Mom quietly says, as if to herself.

This is more a revelation than a question. No answer is needed.

"Where does that leave you? Any ideas what's next? Why is he doing this? Is there one for me?" Mom's questions are firing off faster than I can answer them.

"I came here before my next stop. I wanted to see if you'd want to come with me. If it's too hard, I understand. I felt bad enough waiting this long to tell you, so I told myself I wouldn't continue until you and I talked."

"Well, thank you for finally filling me in. Needless to say, I am a bit in shock. I am at a loss for words, and I also have a million things to say, all at the same time. But yes, I'd like to go with you. Where are we going?"

"You helped me again with this one. I had forgotten all about my pet fish and the fish sharing the same name as the eagle until you reminded me. I think where we should go is our old house, to the maple tree, and look for where we buried the pictures I drew of Durana."

"That sounds like something Dad would do," Mom says softly.

I am having a hard time reading her emotions. She seems happy and sad, surprised and comforted, all at the same time. She looks like she has so much to say, as her eyebrows are raised high on her forehead. But she is staring into space with such a blank look, I'm afraid I've lost her attention.

"Okay, well, if you're ready, we can head over there now and start digging. I brought Cozette's beach shovel with me; it's in the car."

Mom responds with something I didn't see coming. "The only problem is, we're going to the wrong place."

CHAPTER 38

MARTY

In the box were plenty of mushy greeting cards to and from each of the Shores and many tickets.

But damn it! None of these tickets are worth the paper they're printed on. I really thought I had it. I thought this was it! I know I've seen Tom's lotto numbers called, and I am sure he knows it too. I would walk into work some mornings thinking, *This is the day Tom will tell me his big, exciting secret*. But that time never came. I was hoping against all hope that I would find a free ticket to an early, luxurious retirement. My ticket to never having to work again. My ticket to freedom and a life of luxury.

I will have to try again. The winning ticket—and I *know* there is a winning ticket—is in that house. I will just have to keep looking. If I have to turn that house upside down, I will.

In the trash, these go.

CHAPTER 39

KRISTY

"What do you mean, 'We're going to the wrong place'"? Funny how she found out about this twenty seconds ago and already has an opinion. Meanwhile, I've been wracking my brain since I found the miniature eagle behind the rock in the park. And Mom hears about my quest this past week and seems to know where to go, or not to go, next.

"Well, our old neighbor, Mary, said the new owners recently redid the entire yard. She sent me pictures, and the *only* thing that remains the same is the maple tree. The whole yard was completely dug up. But more importantly, before we moved, Dad took every single sentimental thing from the house and yard. He even put maple seedlings into cups of dirt and replanted them here. We now have many special trees in our yard. I highly doubt he would've left them. Is there anywhere else you can think of where he would've put them?" Mom declared, as if proud to be contributing to my quest.

"They're clearly not in your freezer, like Joe suggested, so I can't think of anywhere else that would be obvious," I answer.

"I don't think Dad's intention with this scavenger hunt was to be obvious. You know him better than that. He wants you to think outside the box and use that creative brain of yours. But this is your department, not mine. If you can't figure it out, I never will," Mom admits.

"You're right. My thought is it has to be in a freezer. If not buried, a freezer might be a good second choice. Remember how funny he thought it was that Joe suggested we freeze the dead fish so it didn't get eaten by birds? That conversation stuck in my head because I thought it was so disturbing that we would put Durana in a block of ice and see her whenever we went in to get ice cream. But Dad and Joe thought it was hilarious. I'm checking your freezer."

We leave Dad's office and head downstairs to inspect the freezer. I am not getting my hopes up that I will find anything—we've probably been in that freezer at least one hundred times, just in the last month alone.

Of course, not knowing what I'm looking for, I empty the entire contents of the freezer.

Aside from many packages in freezer bags of unidentifiable meats and four dozen apple cider donuts covered with freezer burn, there seems to be nothing out of the ordinary.

As much as I want to toss all this stuff, I am not here to clean out her refrigerator and freezer; I am on a mission and cannot get sidetracked.

Nothing here. Should I tackle the fridge? No part of me wants to attempt that. I can't even imagine the number of expired casseroles that have taken up residence there. Plus, never did Joe suggest "refrigerating the dead fish."

"Hey, Mom, is your old refrigerator in the garage still plugged in?" When we hosted holiday dinners, the only way Mom managed to keep everything cold was the garage refrigerator. It was the worst job when Mom would say, "Kristy, would you run out and grab the ham? And Joe, grab the turkey, and Sandra, can you bring in the sweet potatoes?"

It was especially horrible when it was cold or raining. I shouldn't be complaining about these kinds of problems, but an attached garage would have been helpful in times like these. There is no way Mom could've hosted without the extra fridge.

"Sure, it's always plugged in. Dad liked to keep his beer in there for when he was working in the garage." She looked at me like I was onto something.

We both hurried out back to the garage.

Sadly, the refrigerator had only one lowly six-pack of beer, and the freezer was empty.

Quite sad, really.

The ice cube bucket was the only thing in the vacant freezer. With one giant block of ice, which froze and melted, then refroze, then melted and refroze again. I suppose every time the power went out, no one bothered to clean out the garage fridge. It always went forgotten.

I pulled what seemed to be a tray of a two-ton ice block out of the freezer.

It was completely cloudy and unusable. I brought it to the driveway and turned the bucket over, hoping to at least clean out the tray. The block was totally stuck to the tray. A stick nearby should do the trick in loosening up this nasty ice. Not that anyone would ever use it, but I just can't imagine there being a benefit to leaving it in there.

It's not budging. Mom has a kettle on the stove with the remains of her boiled tea water; I will try that as my last attempt at cleaning out this tray.

I take the kettle outside to the driveway, where I've left the ice tray, and pour it over the block of ice. It is so satisfying to watch the exterior of the chunk melt. The block melts away from the tray and now easily slides out onto the blacktop driveway. As the cloudy ice starts turning to water, I notice what looks like plastic in the middle of the ice block.

A huge smile fills my face, and I look around to see who I can tell that I think I've found something.

Remembering that Mom went in the house to grab an afghan and never came back out, I go inside to heat up more water. "Mom, you deserted me too soon. I think I'm onto something!"

"Oh really!? You found something from Dad?" I think she is in disbelief that Dad is still so present in our lives. I can't help but notice how distracted she's been lately. But I am too focused to harp on that; there will be plenty of time when the hunt comes to an end to dwell on this journey and what it took to get here.

The kettle heats up quickly, and Mom joins me outside with a look of confusion on her face.

She watches me as I carefully pour the hot water onto the ice. Slowly but surely, the frozen block finally becomes a puddle of water, leaving behind a freezer bag with something inside. Something inside, just for me. I have found what I was looking for!

CHAPTER 40

"Honey, before you continue, I realize these moments are for you and Dad. I'd be lying if I said I wasn't shocked, overwhelmed with emotion, and completely disappointed that you didn't tell me right away. You lied by omission about something so important. But I do appreciate you eventually bringing me into it; you have no idea how much I appreciate it. I also know that Dad addressed these letters to you, so if you'd like to read them first and then share them with me, I will understand. And in the meantime, it is getting late. How about I pick up Cozette and take her out for something to eat on our way home? It'll give you some time here alone, if that works?"

Wow, I really can't believe how understanding Mom is about all of this. All I wanted to do was keep this between Dad and me, but of course, I felt so guilty. I hope Sandra and Joe are as understanding as Mom is when I finally tell them.

Mom heads out to school pickup, and I bring my newest found treasure inside to enjoy in the warmth of their home.

It seems like a long walk from the garage to the back door. Every task now feels like it's in slow motion: opening the door, taking off my shoes, getting comfy on the couch. These mundane tasks that I do every day and don't think about are taking on a life of their own, since I am so anxious to open this bag.

Finally settled in, I begin to open the bag. It is a plastic bag inside another plastic bag. I'm glad to see how cautious he was when planting this clue in water; it would be devastating if, after all of this, the clue were illegible and smeared because it didn't stay dry. When I retrieve the contents of the bag and unfold it, it brings me back to the '90s and drawing these pictures. I suspected it would be the pictures and letter to Durana, but that is all I expected to find.

I'm pleasantly surprised to see that I was wrong!

As I read my letter to Durana and look at the pictures, I notice an extra page, one that doesn't match the others. It is clearly newer and much more recently added than my one of the fish.

I carefully unfold the paper. Although it was protected by the Ziploc bags, who knows how long it's been in here? I do not want to rip it in my haste.

My dad's writing. Oh, how I have never loved my dad's writing as much as I do now!

The rush of finding what he has left for me is just as exciting as seeing what he wants to tell me. He and I really were a good team. He always said we should go on the *Amazing Race* together. He even went as far as to print out the application but then stopped short when it listed all the vaccines, tests, and requirements that were needed before even applying. He said it seemed like a lot of work to not even be guaranteed a spot on the show. That's where our *Amazing Race* aspiration ended.

"Hey Kiddo! Wow, you really are good at this, and it certainly isn't getting easier.

Obviously, I'm not sure how long this is taking you, but something tells me you're flying right through it. And if I know you, you haven't even had to ask anyone for help. You were always wise beyond your years, in both book smarts and common sense!

I assure you, all this creative thinking and effort will most certainly pay off in the end.

Keep going!

First, does this stone mean anything to you? And when you think of it, what is your most memorable time IN it?

OOO!
Dad"

Attached to the letter is a small ring. A ring I don't recognize. Should I? I think I would remember it if it were mine. I don't even think this belonged to Sandra. I've never seen it.

It is a simple silver band with one small ivory stone.

What is sentimental about ivory? Soap? Elephants? Neither?

Maybe it's a birthstone? Could this stone be someone's birthstone? I'll check online. Oddly enough, I don't even know my own birthstone, let alone the other eleven months of the year.

Hmm, garnet, amethyst, emerald, citrine, whatever that is, but no ivory.

This stone may not actually be ivory; it's more iridescent than ivory.

Opal. This is an opal.

The first car I remember my mom having was a Buick Opal.. I loved that car; I'm not sure why. I just remember I loved talking about the story of that car, which is probably why it sticks in my mind as such a core memory. My grandpop, my mom's dad, won the car at our annual St. Rose Christmas Bazaar in the early '90s. Nobody I knew ever won anything, before or after that big score. I remember all of us grandkids screaming in excitement, and my grandpop not looking all that happy. He leaned over to my grandma and said, "I bought tickets as a donation; I had no intention of winning. Now I'll have to pay taxes on it."

Hence, the car is being gifted to my mom. I remember them talking about giving it to Mom because she needed a new car and avoiding having to pay into a higher tax bracket, whatever that meant at the time.

All I knew was we had a new car, and it was a great story.

My mom drove *everywhere*. Every carpool, every errand, every play-date, every beach trip, Mom was always driving. That car went on so many adventures and could tell so many stories. But the one I remember most is stalling on the side of the road after Mom flooded the engine one hot afternoon. We had to let the engine sit for a bit to let the excess fuel evapo-rate. It felt like an eternity sitting on the curb in the heat, just waiting. It's also hard to believe that, as kids, we knew not to complain of boredom. No phones, no tablets, just me and my siblings sitting under an overpass to be in the shade while waiting. I'm sure we kept busy collecting rocks or something, but what sticks out in my head is waiting underneath the train overpass and feeling it vibrate and tremble above us when trains passed.

As I catch myself lost in deep memories, I snap to. Is this stone in fact an opal? Could Dad possibly be talking about the time we stalled? Because of all the great places we went to in that car and all the family vacations that the Opal took us on, what I remember most is the time it stalled. And how amazing my mom was at handling what could have been very dramatic for three little kids. I remember looking at her, thinking, *Wow, nothing rattles my mom. She can be calm, which makes me feel calm and safe in just about any situation.*

It seems like a bit of a stretch, but I have nothing to lose. Mom is giving me a little wiggle room by taking Cozette to eat while I figure things out. Now is as good a time as ever. I really do not remember the exact loca-tion of the stall. But what I do know is it was by a train underpass in Haddonfield. I'm sure there are no more than three or four options in total to choose from. I'll keep looking until I find the right one.

I'll just text Leo to tell him the latest. Then I'll be on my way.

CHAPTER 41

Unlike the previous challenges, I would really like to figure this one out within a day. The others have gone over the span of a few days, and I'm really getting anxious to see what information the next clue holds for me.

What if there is some kind of expiration date on this? What if someone finds a clue that Dad has left for me? What if he didn't bring the bag containing Durana drawings to the new house? They would've surely been tossed during the renovation. Or worse yet, what if they cut the maple down while constructing their new backyard? The clues would have been over before they began. The way I look at it, I've been very lucky so far, but time is wasting, and the faster I get through this, the more likely I'll succeed.

All of this is going through my head as I drive toward the Speedline station in Haddonfield.

I start at the beginning and head east. Driving down Atlantic Ave. seems to make the most sense, as it runs parallel to the tracks. Seems easy enough at first, but these streets seem to be mostly *one-way,* and unfortunately, not in the direction I am going. I get off course a bit, but continue to keep my eye on the direction of the tracks.

At one point, I hit a dead end and get out of my car to see what I can from where I stand. I have driven most of the tracks that go through Haddonfield, and I'm beginning to think I should regroup and start over.

When I reach the fence lining the dead end, a train happens to whiz by. My eyes follow it to see a bridge less than a block from where I stand. I put my car in park and take my keys. At this rate, it'll be quicker to run down the grassy hill toward the road with the underpass than to navigate by car.

I run down the hill, my feet barely touching the ground. I can already tell before even making it to the road that this is exactly the place. I can almost envision the Opal stalled by this very underpass. I can now remember it like it was yesterday. We rolled down this hill while we were waiting for the Opal to start again. Laughing and racing, without a care in the world.

I reach the spot, out of breath. It is a cold day, and I am not dressed appropriately. A T-shirt and three-quarter zip are not keeping me warm enough. But I'm not about to turn back now.

I look around for anything that will remind me of Dad. Nothing yet, but he wouldn't make it that easy. He knew I love a great challenge.

There are just some puddles in the road and a hubcap leaning on the curb; otherwise, it's desolate. Neither of which has anything to do with him. Let me sit like I did many years ago, while waiting for the engine in the Opel to dry out so Mom can start the car and take us home. After all, I had sat on the bench in the park, and I had been taken back to the moments lost in my memory, which may possibly work here too.

A few cars whiz by, and I'm wondering if this is the safest idea. Did Mom really let us sit here and hang out while waiting? I know I would have Cozette sitting buckled up in her car seat with all the car doors open and hazard lights on, just so she'd be safe. That is the biggest difference between my generation and the Baby Boomers: they allowed their kids so much more freedom. We could explore and play outside all day by ourselves as long as we were home for dinner. Kids now are on a very short leash—which I am sure will bite them in the ass when they try to survive the real world on their own.

As I sit here, I can't help but reminisce about my childhood and all the fun we had with the freedom we were provided. All week, I have been saying, "I need to do more of that," and this is no exception.

More freedom for Cozette to discover and explore is probably item number ten of the things I've taken away from this experience. Until then, this underpass needs my attention.

I look closely at my surroundings. Not a single bit of graffiti, nothing at all out of the ordinary. I check out the sidewalk more closely. Aside from some kids engraving into what was, at one point, fresh concrete, there's nothing strange. This looks like a patch of newer concrete than the rest of the sidewalk. I bend down to see what the engravers had to say.

KLS JFM 270 N 85* E*

"THESE ARE MY INITIALS! THIS IS FOR ME!" I scream for no one to hear.

But *JFM*? Followed by coordinates? Maybe they will come to me, but for now, I know this is for me.

Looking harder, I see worn-out shapes next to my initials. A square and a triangle are drawn above it. The only thing I can think this could be is a house. My dad used to tell us that a house was the most fun thing to draw. It's just a square with a triangle above it for a roof. And then the fun part: time to express our creative abilities! We would all start with the square and triangle and then compare the pictures when we were finished to see how differently our minds perceived the perfect home.

But where could these coordinates be leading me? And where am I starting from? It wouldn't be here; that would be too obvious for anyone to follow. I know it isn't here, but where? A house, I assume. Mom's house? Possibly. That's definitely a good starting point.

I take a picture of the sidewalk and head back to my car to first figure out where to start, then I will follow these coordinates. Looks like if I plan to keep going, I'll be tracking down these coordinates in the dark. I just really don't want to wait another day.

∽

Up the five flights I go to my apartment. Leo and I cannot move in together soon enough. I would love to have a nice big house with a huge backyard for Cozette and possible siblings to play with. But not with my waitressing salary, so some things will have to change before that happens.

As I go to slide my key into the lock, I can hear Cozette and Mom giggling. Man, I really am lucky. Like, really, really lucky.

Before I head into what will be chaos, I quickly text Leo. *"Hi sweetie! I'm just getting home from my day of hunting for clues. Come over for dinner, and I can tell you all about it. Love you!"*

I crack open the door and hear, "Mommy's home!" There is no better welcome home than that.

Cozette runs over and jumps into my arms, telling me all about her day, most of it revolving around how Fudge is finally feeling better. Although I'd love to hear about preschool and what she learned and who she played with, I'll take this Fudge conversation with a smile. I really missed Cozette today. My days have been exceptionally busy since Dad's funeral. I just hope she isn't feeling neglected. I will completely focus on her until she goes to bed, and only then will I divulge my latest findings to my mom.

"Mom, I realize it's getting late. Thank you so much for being with Cozette while I took care of some things. Do you have time to stay and hear about it after Cozette goes to bed?"

"I'd love to, but you know how I feel about driving in the dark. And Marty is probably over already; he said he's dropping off some of my dishes that he has. I've been giving him some of my excess food, so it doesn't go to waste."

"Oh, of course. Yes, it's getting dark. Get yourself home, and we can talk about it later."

"Maybe you can call me tonight after you put her down?" Mom suggests.

"Yeah, that's fine. But wait, Marty is just sitting outside in his car until you get back? I feel bad for not letting you know I'd be later than I planned." I feel the need to explain, having no idea Mom had plans after watching Cozette.

"No, honey, it's fine. He'll go in and put the dishes away, I'm sure."

"Wait, why does he have a key?"

"Your dad gave Marty a key many years ago when we went on vacation so he could bring in the mail and water the plants. Since then, we just told him to keep it in case of emergencies."

"Oh. I'm not sure what kind of emergency would require Marty to come over, but whatever."

Mom's shoulders drop, and her eyes begin to tear up. I have no idea why. "Mom, is something wrong? Have I said something to upset you?"

"I'm fine, Kristy. I don't know what's come over me. As I said, just call me after you put Cozette to bed. I can't wait to hear the latest on your quest."

Mom looks completely defeated, an appearance of sadness mixed with an uncertain look of guilt consuming her face. She looks like she has the weight of the world on her shoulders. I've noticed the strain on her face lately, but I assumed it was the grief of losing Dad; now I'm not so sure.

With that, we say goodbye, and I turn to Cozette to play with her. Looks like I will not be following the coordinates tonight like I had hoped.

CHAPTER 42

I end up unexpectedly falling asleep in Cozette's bed while singing to her at bedtime. And that is where I wake up seven hours later. I must've really needed that good night's sleep since I didn't wake once. I slept soundly until this morning when I woke up with a little foot in my face. Cozette is a thrashy sleeper, always found in the opposite position and direction in the morning as to how I left her.

I try to quietly exit her bedroom to brush my teeth and make a cup of coffee while it is still calm and quiet in the apartment. I check my phone to find both a good night and a good morning text from Leo. I text him to come over so I can tell someone about the ice and the underpass. I'm busting at the seams, and I fell asleep before reaching out to Mom.

He responds right away with *"OK, breakfast sandwiches?"* Of course, I'm making him breakfast sandwiches. He knows how much I love feeding him.

Within fifteen minutes, he is at my apartment eating a sandwich, drinking coffee, and listening to my stories.

"I still can't believe you knew to look in the freezer with the clue of a bronze eagle. I just don't get it."

Giggling, I say, "I can't believe it took me *so long* to look in the freezer, to be honest with you. Your mind just doesn't work that way. Sometimes you're too left-brained for your own good," I say as I'm massaging his shoulders.

"Excuse me?" Leo questions my assumption.

"It's not a bad thing, sweetie. You think of everything logically, in black or white. You know, creativity and thinking outside the box are not your strong suit. That's why we're so perfect together. You keep me grounded, and I keep you fun!" I say with a laugh. A subtle smile flickered across his face.

"And from there, a ring turned into an underpass? Maybe you're right about me being too left-brained. Or maybe you're too right-brained. I'd still be looking at the first note from your desk, scratching my head. Either way, you may be right. I think our extreme brains are perfect for each other." With that, he gives me a kiss.

"So, what's next? Figuring out who JFM is? Or tracing those coordinates? And from here? From the underpass?" It seems Leo is really getting into this, which certainly makes it more fun for me.

"I'm guessing this can't go on forever. Dad obviously had a reason for all of this. And he thought to do it before he unexpectedly passed. I'm just hoping that he finished whatever he started and doesn't leave me hanging for the rest of my life." I had been thinking this, but it now feels like a very real possibility, having said it out loud.

"I think I'll try the coordinates first. I went through everyone I could think of that we know and came up with zero people having those initials. *Zero.*"

"I'll try calling Mom and asking her, but in the meantime, I want to try the coordinates from my apartment," I tell Leo as I'm flipping eggs.

"We can certainly try following these from here, but you know your dad thought this living arrangement was very temporary for you. I doubt he would do a scavenger hunt, with a lot of moving parts, from a non-permanent home. I say we try your mom's house. Or even your first family home, but not here."

That's a very good point. Dad didn't love me living in an apartment with Cozette. He didn't love the fifth-floor walkup. He didn't even like the mailroom; he said not to get my mail at night because no one would hear me if I screamed. Looks like we're ruling out the apartment.

"You are right." I feel like I'm always saying those three words to Leo. "When Cozette wakes up, I'll feed her breakfast, and we can head to Mom's. Maybe she'll have an idea about the initials. Then we can leave Cozette with her while we follow these coordinates."

"Sweetie, it's Saturday. I'm late for the golf course as it is. I have a tee time at 10:00. You'll have to do this without me, unless you feel like waiting until 3:00."

"Waiting? I don't feel like waiting until 7:30 a.m. Plus, I need to be at work at 4:30."

Leo brings me back to reality by reminding me of the day of the week and that most people have nine-to-five jobs, five days a week, and over-scheduled weekends.

"I have the dinner shift tonight, so I'll start working on this clue after dropping Cozette off at Mom's. I'll see how much I can figure out on my own. Hopefully I'll have some answers for you after you're done golfing."

"OK, sounds great. Thanks for breakfast; I have to run." And with a kiss goodbye, out the door he goes.

Cozette, hearing the echo of my loud apartment door, emerges with bedhead from her room.

"Morning, Lovebug. How about some eggs?"

Instead of answering me using her words, she chooses to use vomit. Ugh! This was not part of the plan. Looks as though we now have no plan at all. I clean her and the floor, and put her back to bed before calling Mom to tell her I'm staying home for the day. Poor baby. Nothing looks more pathetically sad than a toddler who's just been sick.

When talking to Mom, I'll inquire about the initials and then ask her to come here this evening for my work shift. Nothing screeches plans to a halt like a sick three-year-old.

CHAPTER 43

"No, I'm sorry, I'm not of any help with this one. I have no idea whose initials JFM could be. But, yes, I *can* be of help with Cozette. What time would you like me over, and will she have had dinner yet?"

I guess if Mom only said yes to one of my two questions, watching Cozette would be the more important of the two. I have taken way too many days off this month. If I plan to make my next rent payment, I need to consider taking some extra shifts, not cutting them.

"I made chicken Divan for you, and Cozette will only have dry toast with jelly or maybe a bagel if she gets her appetite back. Also, I need to be in at 4:30, so could you come over before then?"

"Sure, now that I don't have to stop for dinner, that won't be a problem. Marty is going to clean out Dad's workbench in the basement today. I didn't think you would mind. Before he does, is there anything you'd like to keep?"

Why do I sense sarcasm from my mom when she asks me that?

"Hard to say, as I have no idea what is on the workbench. And why the big hurry? It's like you want to rid the house of any evidence of Dad immediately."

"There is no hurry, sweetie. I just feel like I should take advantage of people offering to help me. I'm sure the offers will come to an end at some point, and then it'll be up to me. Aside from you cleaning out the filing cabinets and helping me with the bathroom, no one has offered to help with a thing, except Marty. Your brother and sister have done nothing but stop by for dinner on occasion. I told Marty when he offered that he could have whatever he wanted from Dad's tools because of all the help he has been giving me," Mom says defensively.

Okay, I understand what she's saying. I get that Joe and Sandra have done nothing except play with Cozette while I've cleaned things out. But I wouldn't have it any other way. If not for my cleaning out his office, I never would have known about whatever it is Dad wants to tell me. I wouldn't have been able to have time with my father after he had left this Earth. And I certainly would not have been able to reminisce without his little gentle nudging for me to do so.

"I understand, Mom. You probably feel abandoned in this. But know that the three of us are here for you any time you need something. You just need to let us know what and when. Remember, this is the first time any of us has experienced such a loss. None of us really knows what to do and what not to do."

With that, we hang up. I still don't know what's on Dad's workbench, but it looks like it's all going to Marty and not the three of us, only because we didn't act fast enough. Talk about frustration.

I suppose if I'm not going to be there daily, helping, I need to relinquish some of this control.

Mom arrives nice and early. Cozette only had one episode of getting sick, but she has definitely been lethargic all day. I do envy the PJs in the afternoon, though. I leave Mom and Cozette snuggling on the couch and head out the door.

Not sure if I'll be able to sleep tonight, having no idea what is on

Dad's workbench. I haven't been on his side of the basement in as long as I can remember.

I decide to stop at Mom's to take a quick look and grab whatever one of us might want. I'll be there anyway, following these newfound coordinates from Mom's as a starting point.

My first thought is to just park and get out my compass, since my time is limited. But this is important. If there is something sentimental and I miss it, I'll never forgive myself.

I drive up to Mom's, and it looks like Marty is already there. I let myself in and immediately notice something is off. Marty's shoes are by the front door. How long does he plan to stay? Without calling out his name, I just wander into the kitchen. Lo and behold, Marty is going through my mom's kitchen drawers!

"What the hell are you doing, Marty?"

He quickly turns around, clearly not expecting company.

"Oh, hey there, Kristy. I am looking for some tape. I am here to help your mom clean out your dad's tools, and I'll need to box them to put them in my car."

Reasonable enough. But why does he look like he just saw a ghost? Maybe because of the way I came in here, accusing him of being up to something. Whatever.

"I'm going downstairs to see if there is anything we would want before you pack it all up."

When I get to Dad's side of the basement, it looks like nothing on the workbench has been touched, at least not to my knowledge. It is still a bit dusty on the surface. I guess Dad hadn't been to his side of the basement in some time, either.

Most of Dad's tools are probably older than he was. They look like they could be antiques; maybe they belonged to his dad. Nothing jumps out at me, and unlike my mom, I will not keep something just to keep it. Leo has all the tools he needs, having been a homeowner for quite some time now. As I am heading back up the stairs, Marty is coming down.

"Find anything worth keeping?" he asks.

"No, but won't you need a box to go with that tape?" Other than the tape he just took from the kitchen, he is empty-handed.

"First, I want to see what I'm dealing with. I have some different-sized box options in my trunk, depending on how much needs to be moved."

Again, a reasonable answer. He just really is too at home here in my mom and dad's house.

CHAPTER 44

After locating the compass app on my phone, I open it and hold it up. I triple-check the photo I took of the engraved concrete.

270° N, 85° E. Let's go!

From the looks of the compass and the Bezel indicator, it appears to have me walking toward Main Street in town. I walk, trying to follow the magnetic needle as best I can while also avoiding walking across people's backyards. This is more challenging than I expected. Of course it is; I would be disappointed in Dad's creativity had it not been challenging.

I have to keep checking the time. I spent a few more minutes at Mom's than I should have, and I really cannot be late for work. It's 3:20, and I have no way of knowing how far I'm expected to follow this thing.

Turning back seems like a reasonable thing to do. I can just get back into my car and try following it for a bit, then, when there is not a minute left to spare, I'll head to work.

I need to make a quick pit stop at Mom's before getting back on my route. I need to talk to Marty.

I walk through the front door as Marty is reaching the landing from the basement. His hands are full of what appears to be a very heavy box.

Much-deserved egg on my face. "Hey Marty. Sorry for snapping earlier. I'm just a bit sensitive when it comes to Dad's belongings. I need to loosen up the reins a bit, or I'll be packing up this whole house myself. So, thank you for helping Mom, and I promise I'll try to be less snarky in the future."

"Oh, no worries, Kristy. I know what you are going through. I've lost both my parents and my wife. It's hard. Really hard. Sometimes I wonder if it's ever going to get easier. I just like to keep busy. Keeping busy helps. If my mind isn't on my project at hand, it'll wander. And my mind wandering isn't good; that's when things start to get depressing," Marty tries to explain while standing in the basement doorway, balancing a heavy box, and blowing hair out of his eyes. This really is a sad sight. I've said my peace; I need to go.

"Okay, I'll be heading out now. If there's anything valuable that I've overlooked, please put it aside for my mom. She'd appreciate that."

"Absolutely, Kristy, consider it done."

Back in the car I go, as the wind is picking up. It's been an abnormally warm December so far in the Northeast. By now, I'd normally be in my heavy-duty gloves, but not so far this year. I haven't even broken out my winter coat yet, and that is unheard of for me.

Where was I? *270* N, 85* E.*

In that general direction I will go, for as long as I can. But I must make 3:40 my hard stop and head to work.

Well, this is unfortunate. It's 3:35 now. "Yippee, five whole minutes," I say out loud to only myself, while rolling my eyes. I suppose I will drive NE for five minutes and continue this tomorrow.

I set out toward my unknown destination. As I suspected, right onto Main Street in town. But how far does he want me to go? I continue by following my compass until 3:40.

Defeated, I looked around and decided that now I'm pushing it. The police station and municipal building are to my right, and John's Market is to my left. I wish I had time to run in for bagels, but there is no way. If I do that, I might as well not even show up to work. *Prioritize*, Kristy. I make a U-turn in the middle of the street only because I am by myself in the car. Absolutely no one is coming in either direction, and I'm about to be late.

Sorry, John's Market, the bagels will have to wait.

CHAPTER 45

I run into the restaurant and see my coworker Colleen covering my shift until I am on the floor. She really is a lifesaver. "Col, I owe you!"

She looks at me and replies, "Again." And walks into the kitchen. Yikes. Yes, again.

I realize I have not been a model employee as of late, but that will turn around quickly. It has to. I need this job until I figure out what I'm doing with my life.

The only thing I know for sure is that I'm marrying Leo, although I have no idea what that wedding will look like, just like I have no idea how or when I'm going to open my restaurant. I have no idea when I'll be able to move out of my apartment. I have no idea how long Mom will want to stay in her house alone; it's certainly more house than she needs. I have no idea what Dad was up to when planting these hints all around. I have no idea where my brother and sister have been. I have no idea about anything.

But it needs to change. That much I do know.

～

I grab the check from my last table after what seems like a five-minute shift, not a five-hour one. Super-busy Christmas shoppers make for a profitable night for me. As I'm hanging up my apron and about to text Mom that I am on my way, it hits me.

As I am going through my mental list of "to-dos," it hits me. Text Mom... put laundry in... Stop at John's Market for cold cuts and bagels... John's Market... John's Friendly Market.

JFM! John's Friendly Market. Of course! That makes total sense! It's in the exact compass line, it has the right initials—it's *it*.

Oh, how I wish it weren't so late. They are most definitely not open. Once again, it will have to wait until tomorrow. But man alive, I can't stop smiling that I figured it out. JFM! Who the heck would know that? Dad's note was right; this is *not* getting easier. "Please let there be a finish line before it gets too hard for me," I say aloud as I start my car.

Quick text to Mom, then on my way home.

I cannot wait to hug my baby girl and see how she's feeling. And tell my mom what I have discovered!

Finally making it to the top step, I see my landlord walking toward me. "Hi, Mrs. Cone! How are you this evening?"

"I'll be much better when I receive your rent for this month."

"Yes, of course. I'll slide it under your door first thing in the morning."

She shuffles by me in her slippers, smelling of cigarette smoke. Why do people still smoke? What is this, the '80s, when we didn't really know how bad it was for us? Plus, she stinks.

I've never been more tempted to take Leo up on his offer to help with my bills. Starting with my rent. But I've always been a big believer in living within my means. And with that, paying my own way. When we are married, I'm sure things will be different, but I feel good knowing I can raise my daughter just fine on my own. Not needing a handout is very important to me. Leo respects that. But that doesn't mean I have not been tempted. This month is one of those times.

Walking into my apartment, I start as if in mid-sentence. Throwing my keys on the kitchen counter, I start in. "Mom, are you ready for this?"

"Yes, I'm anxious to hear. But first, just to let you know, Cozette devoured the chicken Divan you left, so it's safe to say she'll be totally back to normal tomorrow."

"And she told me Fudge got her sick. What an imagination she has; I love it! Oh, I spoke with Marty, and he said you stopped by. Everything okay?"

"He called you?" I hesitated to ask.

"Yes, he had questions about some of the items. He wanted to know if certain tools were important for me to keep. The tools that looked the most worn, he assumed Dad used most, and he didn't want to donate them to the senior center if they were sentimental to me."

"Oh wow, that certainly is thoughtful." Here I thought he wanted to get his hands on something valuable before we had the chance to go through things. Now to find out he's donating to the senior center.

"What did you tell him?"

"Well, I don't think any of the tools will be of use to me. I am certainly not going to learn how to use them at this point in my life. He might as well give them to the center where they need them."

"That's probably best. Now, are you ready to hear about my day?"

"Do you have some answers?" Mom asks impatiently.

"Well, not exactly *the* answer, but answers nonetheless. I figured out JFM!"

"Oh! Tell me who it is."

"It's actually a what, not a who. John's Friendly Market. Can you believe it? The compass lines up and everything. And, of course, it was closed by the time I got off work. I'm going to head there tomorrow morning to scope it out, and assuming Cozette is feeling better, I'll take her to school on my way."

"It sounds like you have it all figured out! That's great, honey!"

I finish drying the dinner dishes and putting them away. The dish-towel is soaked, so I hang it to dry as I walk over to the couch, still talking to Mom.

"Funny you should say that. I spent most of my work shift literally thinking the opposite. That I have *nothing* at all figured out. But I much prefer your perspective. Dad and I had that positive perspective spin on everything in life. When did that change?"

"Sometimes, you just need to try a little harder to find the good spin. And it can take a bit more creativity to find the positive. But it can always be done. And should always be done."

"Thanks, Mom. I needed that today."

"Okay, well, I'd better be going. You know how I feel about driving in the dark. Your shifts seem to be getting later, and the sun is setting earlier —not a great combo! Hope you did well and made lots of tips tonight!"

"I did; thanks again for watching Cozette. Glad she wasn't sick for you." And out the door she goes.

It leaves me wondering what John's could possibly have for me. Obviously, it wouldn't be anything on the shelves. He wouldn't risk having an important item in this hunt being purchased and in someone's pantry right now. Lord knows how long it could've taken me to get this far. It would have to be something that is more of a permanent fixture. I could rack my brain all night, but it could be a complete waste of time. I'll have to see what John's has for me first thing in the morning.

A quick goodnight peck for Cozette, and I'll turn in myself. As much as my ears are ringing right now from being in a loud, crowded bar, the best thing for me would be to lie down and try to get a good night's sleep. Leo has been in his bed and, therefore, sound asleep for hours. So, there's really nothing keeping me up. I should take advantage of this rare night with nothing to do. A nice hot shower, and I'm turning in.

First order of business tomorrow: talking to the ladies at John's. I'll tell them everything and see if they know how to assist me. It certainly can't hurt, and I really need to get to the bottom of this.

CHAPTER 46

With our rushed and hectic morning, my first exhale is when I see Cozette walking in the single-file line into the school building with Mrs. Lauren, thanking my lucky stars that she did a complete 360 and feels great today.

I tear away from that school like I just robbed a bank. This is exciting. What does John's have to do with my dad, and will this be my last stop? I'm torn between busting at the seams with excitement and not wanting this fun adventure to end. I pull up to John's and sprint across the street, beating the crossing guard to his midstreet post.

Bursting through their ancient swinging door, I'm out of breath. I really do need to start working out. "Hi, ladies!" I practically sing out to them. There is a small line. It's best not to be rude and just start talking, so I begrudgingly get in line too.

Finally, the sweet old men in front of me take their bagels, cold cuts, and lottery tickets and exit the store so painfully slowly.

My turn! "Hi again, ladies!"

"My, you're awfully chipper this morning!" one of the workers notices and comments on all the coffee I've had already this morning.

If this store has been here since 1918, these women have likely been here since 1919. It's awesome.

"I'm in a very interesting situation." I start the shortened explanation, as I would like to get the important details out before the line forms again. It's one thing to share with the staff because they may know something, but I would rather the entire town not be in on this yet; I mean, my siblings don't even know. Wouldn't that be a hoot if Sandra found out from Mary down the street? Yeah, I'd better mention to the ladies to keep this to themselves.

Once I am done with the Cliff Notes version of what I've been up to the past week or so, I seem to have their utmost attention. They've even been ignoring the line that is starting to grow.

"How about you take care of these customers? I'm in no hurry. We can continue when it slows down again."

The elderly man first in line looks over at me as if to ask if I'm done talking yet and he can have his turn with the checkout ladies. "Can you believe it's mid-December already? I haven't figured out this 'shopping online' craze, so I'll be heading to the mall this week to knock out my shopping list."

If one more person asks the women if they're ready for the holidays, I'm going to scream. Of course they're not! No one ever is! Let me guess, "How did it get here so fast?!" "Where did December go?" "Wasn't it just Thanksgiving yesterday?"

Et cetera, et cetera, et cetera.

Finally, my turn again. "OK, so, I'm not sure if you can be of any help to me. But I guess I'm looking for anything out of the ordinary or something that would be meaningful to my dad. I know you all knew him, but I'm guessing he never mentioned any of this to you or left anything with you?"

"Honey, I'm sorry, he didn't. But oh, how we adored your father. What a nice man. And such a sad day when we heard about the accident."

"Yes, so sad," another woman chimes in. I believe she is the daughter of the original owner, John. If not for this being her family business, she would have retired by now. "Go ahead, sweetie, and take all the time you need looking around. Let us know if we can help in any way."

"Thank you! I will be a while because I'm not sure what I'm looking for... but I'll let you know if I uncover anything."

Fortunately, Colleen agreed yet again to take my shift today, so I really do have nothing but time. Time, and heaps and heaps of laundry. But that can wait. This needs to be my priority right now because if I keep giving out my shifts at work, there won't be work.

I start by walking up and down each of their four aisles.

I am fairly certain that I won't be finding anything in an aisle, but it seems like a good place to start. Nothing in produce, nothing in pasta, nothing in cookies and cereal, and nothing in paper products. Maybe the deli? That is what this market is known for: fresh deli meats and bagels. They still have the same worn wooden block as they did when I was little and probably when my parents were little. But I can't see how anything back here would be for me. The turnover of these products is so fast, I'm guessing it would be impossible to plant something back here in the deli.

Now it's time to try outside. They have a big table for the spring and summer months, which always holds the best Jersey tomatoes and corn on the cob. Of course, it being December, it's empty now. But let me look just to be sure.

Nothing.

Outside the left side of the door is a take-one-leave-one free library. Doubtful anything could be there, and if there was, it's likely in someone's home as we speak. Not much good that would do me.

I head back in, not even close to giving up.

"Nothing inside or out as far as I can tell," I let the women know.

"Feel free to take a seat and give this some thought if you'd like. And take as long as you need," John's daughter pleasantly announces. I'm thinking this may be the most unique, out-of-the-ordinary thing that has happened here in some time.

I take her up on her offer and collapse into the offered folding chair. This random chair in the middle of the store probably gets used more than it doesn't. I think, based on the average age of the customers, it's probably a welcome addition to the store. I'll just sit and observe for a bit. See if anything pops into my mind.

I watch the checkout ladies as they talk to every single customer who walks in and out. No wonder it's named John's Friendly Market. They know everyone by name, which explains all the Christmas cards, baby announcements, and kids' drawings hanging all over the front counter and beams throughout the store. I've never seen a more loyal fanbase for any store.

I've been sitting long enough, and I've also been getting eyed up by the elderly man in the bread section. Thinking he is waiting to sit, I say, "It's all yours, sir. I was just taking a little break."

Back up and down the aisles I go, but this time, I'm reading the hanging cards.

Some of these cards are ancient. Most are yellowed and have curled-up corners. A few are so old that the penned signature is all but worn off. So far, I've seen baby announcements from two different classmates of mine. *Their* baby announcements, not those of their own children. Many of these are over thirty years old. It's like a time machine in here. And I have seen so many families of classmates and old neighbors; it looks as if every family in town has, at one point or another, dropped a card off to John's.

Up high on the center beam is a card with my old grammar school, St. Rose, decorated for Christmas. I've never seen this card, so again, it's probably well before my time.

I stand on my tippy-toes to read the inside of the parish card. This cannot be.

It's signed:

"Happiest of Holidays to all at John's,
...our favorite market!
~ Mr. and Mrs. Shore and our newest addition, Kristy"

CHAPTER 47

Before taking the card off the column, I exclaim my finding to the ladies. "Ladies! This is it! It must be!"

"What did you find, dear?" the oldest woman asks.

"There is a card signed by my dad hanging on the post over there! Mind if I take it down?"

"Of course, we don't mind! It's yours. Think it will help you solve this mystery of yours?"

"I'm sure it's why I'm here, but I don't know yet what it means. When I figure it out, you'll be the first to know."

I grab the card and head out of the store. I'm sure I have what I need, so there's no reason to linger any longer. First, I call Leo to tell him what I've found, and next, Mom.

Leo is curious and excited to hear about my latest quest. But Mom is over the moon. She forgot all about that card and insists I come over to her house with it on my way back to my apartment.

Before pulling away, I text Leo, having forgotten to ask him earlier about our standing Wednesday night date. I pray that he doesn't have another holiday dinner or Christmas party. It is overdue that we get back on schedule with my favorite night of the week. Things have been a total whirlwind these past weeks, and we need to get back into some normalcy and back to a routine, for all our sakes.

He responds immediately, *"Yes! I've been waiting to get you back on our Wednesdays!"*

∾

Turning over the card for the first time, I see Dad has written just two words: *"Same year."*

∾

I pull into Mom's driveway, and for the first time in a while, Marty's car is not here. Nice. I would like to spend a little alone time with Mom without lingering ears in the background. Not that he is necessarily up to anything nefarious, but it wouldn't be fair if he knew more than my siblings. It's time to tell them. No excuses.

I walk into Mom's, and she's on the phone. It's like she's making up for the time lost by not having a cell phone for the first sixty years of her life and has a lot of catching up to do. People of that generation are funny: old enough to not rely on cell phones because almost all of their lives have been without them, but downright giddy with every call they receive because they know how amazing technology can be. And I do feel bad about interrupting her call, but this is important.

"Mom, we need to talk. Can you call them back?"

Mom looks at me and turns away. "Yes, I'll call you back. Kristy just got here, and she has some details for me. Okay, yes, that sounds good! See you then."

And with that, she turns back around. "Tell me, what did you find?"

"Um, okay, right. I went to John's, and after some intense looking around, I found this."

I hand her the Christmas card, which was originally delivered about thirty years ago.

"Oh my! I had forgotten all about this card!"

"But you do remember it?"

"Well, not *exactly*, but now that I see Dad's handwriting, I remember how he delivered cards when he took his walks. And I know he and John were buddies, so it doesn't surprise me that he delivered a card to John at the market."

Wow. This is like a cool little glimpse into Dad's life as a young man that I really don't know much about.

I'm feeling guilty and extremely selfish right now for not asking him more questions about his life. For much of my life with my dad, it was all me, me, me. Drive me here. Buy me that. Help me with this. I need to borrow money, etc.

Sure, all kids are that way, and most of them realize that life with parents is not forever. I will probably live more of my life without my parents than with them. Looking at it that way makes me want to cry. All of the things I would have done differently, all of the problems I would have solved on my own, and all the help I would've given them. Had I known my time with my dad was so limited, I probably would have had a notebook and pen with me each time I visited.

I can almost picture him pushing a baby carriage with me as a little baby sleeping inside, delivering Christmas cards to all his local friends. Hard to believe he was my age then!

"Mom, do you know what this card and 'same year' might mean? I haven't given it much thought yet, but before I start racking my brain, does anything pop out at you?"

Mom looks off into the distance, deep in thought.

"It doesn't, no. It could be written inside the card what you have to do next, and I'd probably still be confused."

That is precisely why Dad and I loved doing word games and challenging puzzles together—Mom had zero interest.

"Okay, let's think about it. And in the meantime, let's call Joey and Sandra. They still know nothing about this, and I'm feeling guilty for not bringing them into it last week," I confess.

"If I were you, I would not feel guilty. Have they reached out to you at all?" she asks.

191

"No, but they don't know that Dad left me a letter. In their worlds, everything is going along like it normally does. Well, our new normal anyway."

"That doesn't make it right, Kristy. They haven't reached out to me either. I realize they lost their father, but I lost my husband. The man I devoted almost forty years of my life to. I've never felt more alone, and they haven't reached out in days, let alone stopped over to see how I'm doing. I know they are very caught up in their own lives right now, but they should know better. They should be making sure their mom is okay."

Mom putting it that way makes me wonder if I've done enough. But it also makes me feel a heck of a lot less guilty about not yet telling Joey and Sandra.

"Mom, should we call them on speaker so we can both talk?" Suddenly I'm feeling much more confident.

"Sure, let's start with Joe," Mom suggests.

Good idea, since he will likely ask no questions, and his call will be much faster than Sandra's.

As Mom predicted, on and off with Joe. No questions, no details requested. "No way! Really?" was about all we got from him. At least it was easy.

Now for Sandra.

"Hey, Sandra! It's Kristy and Mom on speaker from my phone."

"Oh no, what is this about? Why are you calling me together? What happened?"

"It's not bad, don't worry," Mom assures her.

"Yeah, Mom's right, not bad at all. Pretty exciting, actually."

"Go on..." she impatiently asks.

"When I was cleaning out Dad's office, I found something."

"Oh God, do I even want to know?" I can almost hear her rolling her eyes through the phone. She no doubt thinks I ran into a snag of some sort and am asking her for her help. Now I perform the eye roll.

"Don't know. But we're telling you anyway." I am just about at my patience threshold.

"I found a letter addressed to me in one of Dad's desk drawers. It was a game of sorts, kind of like a scavenger hunt. But I haven't figured out the point yet. I've been finding clues though, and it's been very exciting, like a piece of him is still here with us."

"Wait a minute. So, you're telling me Dad wrote you a note. You opened this said note, have been searching for clues from Dad, and are just telling me now? What did he leave me?"

And there it is. The youngest child's "Where's mine?" syndrome.

"Sandra, as far as I know, there was no letter for you in Dad's office. You are more than welcome to look, but from what I saw, it was just this one."

I look at Mom and shrug. That's when we lose Sandra's interest.

"I have to go pick up Cozette at school now, so you can call Mom on her cell and continue this conversation. I need to run, bye Sandra."

"No, Kristy, don't you remember? You told me I could pick her up and take her out to dinner. I planned a whole sleepover for us. I want her to still enjoy sleeping over, even though it won't be with Dad," Mom added.

"Okay, why don't you two go figure out your logistics? I have to go anyway. Bye." Sandra interrupts.

And with that, our calls are done, and I am off the hook.

Sounds like Sandra's feelings are a bit hurt. I guess I can't blame her. But if I heard this news from her, I'd want every single detail of what Dad had to say.

That went pretty much exactly as I would've expected. But most importantly, it's done.

Band-Aid ripped off, and now I can focus on this game of life that Dad has gifted me with.

CHAPTER 48

Mom taking care of Cozette may have been a perfect arrangement at one time. Now I feel as though I should be worrying a bit about how long she has to watch her and how late she stays. I'm sure Mom takes the best care of Cozette, and she knows more about parenting than I do at this point, but Mom falling asleep with Cozette on her lap was indeed eye-opening.

I will have to call and text Mom more often than normal just to check on things. And I'll need to find a way to do it that doesn't come off as condescending. I don't think I will be at ease without checking on her a few times up until bedtime.

Only then will Leo have my undivided attention. I cannot wait to be with him. But tonight, no cooking. I want to order takeout, so I have no distractions whatsoever.

One of my favorite things about our Wednesday dinners together is our weekly wrap-ups. Leo and I are like two teenagers in love who are busting at the seams to see each other and have so much to say. He usually gives me most of the airtime, and tonight will be no exception.

I haven't thought too much about the Christmas card from John's, but I need to really put my mind to it. Hopefully, Leo will be able to offer some assistance. An outsider's perspective is always helpful, especially with something like this. I tend to overthink, so if the answer is staring at me in the face, I'm likely to miss it.

I call our favorite salad place and put in our orders. Like many other things in our relationship that are polar opposites, our salad orders are no exception. We both agree on our favorite restaurant for salads and order them often, but wow, the two orders are as different as can be. Leo cringes at my extra olives, and I can't believe anyone could order pasta as a salad topping. After all, they are two completely different main dishes.

Leo lets himself in, still dressed in his work clothes. No one can make a polo look as sexy as he does. Before the salads even arrive, we can barely keep our hands off each other, so I'm thinking not much will get solved until tomorrow.

Another amazing night with my love. My fiancé.

My morning will be super productive. I will make sure of it. Laundry won't do itself, and neither will the food shopping. Then I'm off to my lunch shift. The restaurant is where I have been doing my best thinking lately, so I have high hopes that work will help contribute some answers.

CHAPTER 49

It's days before Christmas, and work is surprisingly dead. Is everyone panicking and running around to all the stores and skipping lunch? Aside from the token work Christmas lunch office party, there are not many tables full, which is good and bad. I need the money, but the free time to think is something I have not had in weeks. I take advantage of the downtime to chill in the employee break room. No one else is back there except Nicole, the bartender, who is rushing from the bathroom to get back to the bar. The bar never has downtime.

A Christmas card from Dad, Mom, and my baby self to John's Market. What could that possibly mean? I brought the card with me in case I had some time to think. "*Same year*" has me baffled.

The only thing that sticks out to me is the picture on the front of the card. St. Rose of Lima School. What a wonderful place to learn. For three kids to go through one institution with no complaints at all is impressive. Everyone seems to complain about everything. Too strict or not strict enough. Challenging curriculum or curriculum is not hard enough. No need for recess or an absolute need for recess, et cetera.

That's what people do all day, every day. And I cannot remember my mom, my dad, or any of us kids complaining about anything except homework. But what kid doesn't do that? St. Rose holds a special place in my heart. And I guess it did for Dad, too.

Since I have a minute, I'll text Mom and see if she thinks St. Rose could be my next—or possibly last—stop.

"It would certainly make sense. Your dad spent every last dime to get you three through Catholic grammar school and high school. He wanted you to not only have a great education, but manners and life skills that go with such a well-rounded environment. He would tell anyone who would listen that sending you to St. Rose was the best decision he ever made. Not to mention, your father was not even Catholic. So, sending you kids to a Catholic school would have been unheard of at that time."

My mom texts like she is talking directly to me. Punctuation and all.

But what I got from that text is that my dad was the most selfless man. What I am learning about him post-life on earth is truly an amazing gift.

"Mom, mind if I get home a few minutes later this evening? I won't be long. I know schools are not open, but I want to take a walk around St. Rose and look around a little bit. I won't be too late, OK?" I text back in response.

She replies with the perfect answer, *"I'll see you whenever you get home."*

CHAPTER 50

I circle my old grammar school, taking it all in. It has been so many years since I've been on these school grounds. What a great nine years I had here. I loved it when all three of us were here at the same time. We had four years of all of us under one roof, and we just loved, on the rare occasion, that we would pass each other in the hallways.

Our favorite nights were the Friday night basketball games from November through February. It was especially fun when Joe was on the starting five in varsity games during his seventh and eighth grade years. Life was so simple then. My biggest concern was which sparkly shirt I should wear to the game, as it was the height of our social lives at the time.

The school grounds are so much more secure than when I went here. Cameras are everywhere on school grounds, a locked gate circles the block, and there is an intercom system to enter the building. None of this was here in the '90s. I'm glad to see the little bubble we grew up in has upped its game to be as safe in today's crazy world as it needs to be.

I'm sure Dad knew going into a school would be off-limits. Outside is where my clue must be. But what has always been here? The flagpole? The bushes and plants?

It is getting dark out, so it's hard to make out any details of the school itself. And I want to get home to relieve Mom. Plus, it may be just a matter of time before a neighbor calls the police after witnessing a creeper lingering on the school grounds.

I decide to head home and come back tomorrow morning. It'll be nice to get home before Cozette is asleep. I'd love to play with her for a bit before her eyelids succumb to their heaviness.

A few short days until Christmas. Other than our Christmas tree, Cozette's stocking, and the holiday tunes that have been blaring in my car, you'd never know it. I didn't do much as far as decorations this year, not even an elf on the shelf. I feel like a bad mom for depriving Cozette of that obligatory elf. What's the saying, ignorance is bliss? This might be the last year that she'll just roll with it, without an opinion of her own. And truth be told, it's been a crazy and unusual holiday season. I think I get a pass this year.

Visiting Santa will put us in the holiday spirit, much like the light show did last week. On our way to see Santa at the mall, we swing by St. Rose. Maybe what I am supposed to see will be a bit more obvious in the daylight, and I'll get to show Cozette where Mommy went to school.

We park in the church lot and walk around the property. It is a lot less creepy seeing someone walking around aimlessly in the daylight than it is in darkness with the flashlight on from their phone.

"So big, Mommy!" Cozette exclaims. The school, although homey, would seem large to a toddler. Three tall stories and a big gymnasium, in addition to a full basketball court and playground outside.

"Slides!" How did I not prepare an answer for Cozette's expected reaction to a slide? Normally, I would've talked about this in the car before even getting out.

Now that she's seen the playground, it'll take extra explaining and convincing to get her back in the car.

"Cozette, remember Mommy said a quick trip to find something? We don't have time now, and you're not dressed for playing outside in the cold. Don't forget, Santa is going to be waiting for us. We can come back to the playground some other time."

She seems satisfied, for now.

I really need to study this building, since it was so hard to make out in the dark. The only thing that embellishes the brick façade is *"ST. ROSE PAROCHIAL SCHOOL 1921."*

1921.

A year. "Same year."

But the same year as what?

These annual visits to Santa are getting more painful. The older Cozette gets, the creepier it feels to be away from me and on this strange man's lap.

Year one, she slept. Year two, it took a minute for the tears to fall, so we got a few cute pics with not quite a smile but a confused look on her face.

This year, though, she's outsmarted me. The tears start to fall while in the long line before even reaching the staging area. We are not about to turn around, especially considering half of the kids in this line are also crying. Oh, the torture we put our kids through for a picture.

This year's photo will be the puffy-eye addition.

CHAPTER 51

"What is our plan for Christmas? I'd say, same as every year? But nothing is the same anymore." Sandra calls the second we get home from our trip to see Santa.

"I know. I hate the thought of new traditions, but what other choice do we have?" I say, while trying not to sound insensitive.

"I don't know. Why don't we just all go away or do something? Give ourselves a gap year until we get our bearings on losing Dad. Start fresh next year." It's starting to sound like Sandra has given this some thought.

"Although a trip *does* sound needed and fantastic, I think Mom will want to stay close to home, not run away. I finally got her to put up her Christmas tree weeks after she normally would. And it probably wouldn't even be up and decorated yet if Leo and I hadn't lugged it up from the basement."

I do take any opportunity I can to remind Sandra and Joe that Mom does need our help. Mom never wants to be a burden, and she is very independent, but that does not mean she is completely self-sufficient, especially after being a team of two for so many decades.

"Talk to Mom about it. Leo, Cozette, and I are up for anything. I just need a home base for Santa to deliver presents to."

"Okay, well Joe won't do anything because he'll have to go to his in-laws for Christmas Eve dinner. That just leaves you, Mom, and me. I'll talk to her, but I'm guessing it'll be 8:00 p.m. mass on Christmas Eve like every year."

If that is the case, it's fine by me. Dad has only been gone for a month. And that month has been a whirlwind. I could use a little normalcy. Sitting on the couch with Leo, in front of the tree, holding a warm cup of coffee, and watching Cozette open presents sounds like heaven. I may suggest to Mom that we do just that before Sandra gets in her ear about a trip.

∼

I can't stop thinking about 1921.

What could have happened that year? "Same year" must be referring to the school's opening. It could've been referring to the year of the actual Christmas card, but it didn't have a year on the card, which isn't difficult to figure out, but for some reason, I feel like the school on the front of the card is somewhat significant. I'll start there, and if I end up at a dead end, I will have a possible plan B to fall back on.

Let's see, Coco Chanel introduced Chanel No. 5 in 1921; we couldn't be going back to that, could we? After all, it *was* the perfume that I wanted to buy Mom when we were little.

The polygraph was invented in 1921. Could he possibly want me to take a lie detector test?

Insulin was discovered in 1921. Luckily, I don't have anyone close to me with diabetes, so that wouldn't be it.

White Castle opened its doors in 1921. That's not it, just because, well, eww.

Lots of options, but sadly nothing that sticks.

∼

When in doubt, call Mom.

I know the answer will be "No idea," but it doesn't hurt to ask. In true form, she picks up before the second ring.

"Hi, Mom! Quick question. Did you figure out if the year 1921 meant anything to you?"

"No, honey, I'm sorry. I just don't know what 1921 could be referring to. And I am not aware of anything that happened in that year."

Figured.

"OK, well, if anything pops into your head, let me know."

"Will do."

CHAPTER 52

WWDD: What Would Dad Do?

Whenever I had a question growing up, Dad would respond the same way, "Let's look it up!" Whether in an encyclopedia or on the office computer, he loved learning and answering all our curious questions, only to come up with more questions stemming from it, to really get our little minds thinking.

That's what I'll do. I'll research all that happened locally in 1921. Dad would be proud. He is in heaven right now, smiling down on me, looking it up.

The flexibility of looking it up means I can do all the research I want while Cozette takes her nap.

The first two things that pop up are huge.

Nineteen twenty-one was the year our county library was established, which is important and significant to our family. My grandmom, my mom's mom, started the children's section of the library in town. Until my grams, it was just an adult library, with no books for kids. My grams had a hand in improving the quality of life of many children in our area.

But also, and I feel as though it may be my next stop, Tavistock Country Club was established in 1921.

Although all things point to the library, I have a gut feeling, and I'm going with my gut on this one. Worst case, I have yet another very strong plan B.

Tavistock Country Club. An elite club two miles from our house that you can only see the inside of if invited by a member. It's not open to the public, so it has an air of mystery around it.

What would Dad's wish be if he were lucky enough to win the lottery? A proper wedding that Mom deserved... at a country club! He was never specific as to which one, but if he had a choice, Tavistock would most likely be it. It's perfect, aside from its years-long waitlist to become a member.

So that is where I am going next. Not as easy as going to John's Market and talking to the ladies, taking my time, lingering, and resting in a chair. This will involve some creativity. And my timing isn't perfect. It's most likely one of the busiest weekends for the country club. The last thing that many moms want to do is cook right before Christmas, so the restaurant is sure to be jammed.

My best chance at holding someone's attention long enough to get any answers would be to wait until at least after dinner hours, which is fine with me. My work schedule is hectic this week due to our proximity to the mall and how busy that is expected to be. Looks like this will have to be put on hold for just a bit.

CHAPTER 53

This afternoon flies by in a blur of wings and beers, which makes me happy because of the tips and the speed at which I get to go home to Cozette and Leo.

I bring home dinner for them, and we sit in front of the TV to watch Christmas Eve on Sesame Street while we eat. The perfect night.

As soon as Cozette goes to bed, Leo and I toast our Tito's and club sodas and flop onto the couch. We talk about my discoveries from today and my confidence in Tavistock Country Club as we wrap presents and sip cocktails.

I haven't given nearly the attention to these gifts that is deserved. Leo and I have already decided not to exchange due to our weekend getaway to Cape May, which now seems like a lifetime ago. And other than Cozette, we only have one White Elephant exchange. I got off pretty easy this year.

Leo still seems to think that my next stop is the library and that I'm way off. He may be right. He usually is. But my gut is telling me differently.

We will know for sure tomorrow. Although tomorrow, compared to every other stop, I have to say, I am not confident. Between the lack of certainty and my overall discomfort being thrown into a place I've never been, things could go terribly wrong. I keep asking myself what I have to lose. My dignity is all I keep coming up with.

~

Up and dressed and making breakfast sandwiches, I finish my second cup of coffee. "Leo, do you want to stay here with Cozette while I run over to the Club, or should I get Mom, so you can come with me?"

"You know what? Do this on your own, and I'll stay here. I have some computer work to do until she gets up. Then I'll give her the eggs you made, if she's up before you get back."

"Oh, I assure you, she will be up before I get back. She may even be up before I leave," I respond with a long, sensual kiss.

"Okay, well, don't be too long. You cannot kiss me like that and then rush out of here for the afternoon."

~

After a quick shower, I head out the door, trying not to wake Cozette. Success!

Driving over to Tavistock, I ask myself, *Who am I even asking for? What am I supposed to say? Do I valet or self-park? And most importantly, why didn't I insist that Leo come with me?*

No time to answer myself as I pull up to the valet. "Hello, ma'am, here for brunch?"

"Um, no. I just need to speak with someone. Someone in customer affairs, possibly?"

"Customer affairs? I am not sure we have a department called customer affairs. But how about just asking for Catherine? I am sure she will be able to help you with anything you need."

"Thank you...?"

"Paul. The name is Paul. I will keep your car up front; just holler when you're all done."

"Thank you, Paul."

He made it easier than I expected. If the rest of my morning is as pleasant, I will be just fine.

I walk straight ahead to the restaurant and bar, where I am most comfortable.

I ask the bartender where I can find Catherine. Bartenders and wait-staff have a certain understanding. We can spot each other a mile away; it is like we're a team. Maybe it's the way we greet every guest with a welcoming smile, maybe it's the unwavering eye contact, or maybe it's the patience we show each other when we need something. Not sure. But immediately, I feel like he gets me.

"Go upstairs to the main lobby, and her office is the second door on the right. You cannot miss it."

"Thank you so much, Marcus," I say overeagerly as I read the name on his tag. Up the stairs I go, with a sudden rush of confidence. I feel like I am really onto something.

CHAPTER 54

As I walk up the stairs to the main lobby, I can't help but notice how spectacular this place is. Just gorgeous. The Christmas decorations are like nothing I have ever seen. And as intimidating as it is on the outside, it is warm, friendly, and intimate on the inside.

I see two doors upstairs, before the entrance to the formal ballroom. This must be it. The second door is cracked open enough to peek inside.

"Knock knock," I say while knocking. What is wrong with me? Who does that?

"Come in," a pleasant voice responds from behind a desk.

"Hi! You must be Catherine. My name is Kristy Shore. I do not have an appointment, but I was hoping I could ask you a couple of questions."

"You do not need an appointment to see me, unless you are from the local newspaper. Are you from the paper?" Catherine laughs at her own question, as if it's completely absurd.

"Oh no! I am just a regular person, here for personal reasons, not business." Why am I talking like this? Maybe I am more nervous than I thought.

"Okay, regular person, please have a seat. How can I help you?"

I sit across the desk from Catherine in a comfortable mahogany chair cushioned with a maroon leather pillow.

"I don't know if you can, but I am hoping. Long story short, my father passed away last month. I found a letter from him that was intended to be found after he passed, which is weird because he died unexpectedly."

I feel as though I am getting off course here, and I don't want to lose her. I need to get to the point.

"Anyway, my dad left me some puzzles to solve, so to speak. And this Christmas card with a picture of my grammar school is one of them. Written on the back of the card, it just says *same year.* This is supposed to mean something to me, but I am confused as to exactly what.

"Both St. Rose School and Tavistock Country Club were established in the same year, which leads me to believe that this may be the answer, but I'm really not sure. That is where your help would be most appreciated."

"Oh, wow! That certainly is exciting, not to mention extremely thoughtful, but I am not sure of what help I can be." Catherine is doing her best to be patient but looks confused as to why I am here. She begins sorting through her files and straightening up her desk.

"Yeah, so, I am not sure either. I was just hoping that maybe his name, Thomas Shore, would ring a bell, or possibly you would know something. Anything. I brought the card and a picture of my dad, hoping you may recognize him." I gave Catherine a recent photo of Dad and Mom that I grabbed before I left the apartment.

"Would you believe, I actually do. I believe he was in a few months ago. He was interested in renewing his vows with his wife, I am guessing your mom, for their wedding anniversary. It was extremely sweet, but unfortunately, I could not help him. We have a strict sponsor referral system. If you are not sponsored by a member in good standing, you cannot host any type of event in our ballrooms."

While sitting, she turns in her swivel chair to look in her filing cabinet. It is sort of rude. Does she not realize what a big deal this is to me? My dad was right here. He was probably sitting in this very seat just a few short months ago. And he wanted to renew their wedding vows. How sweet is that?

Catherine turns back around, facing me. "Here it is," she says, holding a manila folder. "We keep records of all inquiries, so if and when they receive a sponsorship, we do not have to redo all of the details of said event. It is all right here."

This could be very promising.

"First of all, I am sorry to hear about your father. What a nice man he was."

A moment of awkward silence. Like we weren't sure who was supposed to speak next. Followed by, "Here is his file. It seems he wanted to surprise your mom. He was going to say he made a dinner reservation at our restaurant and then walk into the ballroom, filled with all their friends and family." She continues, "We have never done a surprise vow renewal before. Very sweet."

There is nothing I love more than hearing people's stories of my dad that I do not already know. I am hanging on her every word. Every story shares one common denominator: "He was such a nice man." Everyone agrees on that, which warms my heart.

"May I keep this file?"

"I do not see why not. He never said it was top secret. And possibly it will help you with your guessing game."

Okay, so I don't know if I'd refer to this as a guessing game, but Catherine only knows the little I chose to share, so I won't fault her ignorance this time. After all, she is being quite helpful.

I reach for the folder, hoping it has all my answers enclosed.

Thanking Catherine, I exit her office. I would rather read this in the comfort of my car as opposed to being watched from across a desk.

"Hi Paul, I am ready."

Oh shoot, I don't have cash. I never have cash. Is it rude to ask the valet if he takes Venmo?

"Paul, I'm sorry, I never have cash, and I didn't plan on valeting my car today..."

"No worries, I hope Catherine was able to help you. This one's on me. Have a nice rest of your day!"

My opinion of stuck-up country clubs is out the window. Maybe this will be a New Year's goal for Leo and me: save up for a Tavistock membership.

I'm laughing out loud. What's next? I take up golf?

CHAPTER 55

A nice family dinner is long overdue. I will host tonight and even invite Mom, Joe, my sister-in-law, and Sandra to come. It will be good to get together and not just console each other while we're all in tears.

Now that Mom is getting her appetite back, I will make her favorite: chicken and brie in puff pastry.

But before I even think about going to the grocery store, I am dissecting what is in this envelope.

It is not sealed shut, so the metal clasp opens easily. I pull out the only two pages that are enclosed. It looks like an order form of sorts. The why, where, and when of the event. Dad filled out his home address and phone number but left the date of the event blank.

In the section titled *"Please describe your event,"* Dad stated almost exactly what Catherine did minutes ago.

"I would like the opportunity to renew my wedding vows with my wife of over thirty-five years. She has always dreamed of a country club wedding, but at that time, sadly, it was not in our budget.

"If there comes a time when events do not require being sponsored by a member, please reach out so I may show my wife the wedding she has always deserved, but I haven't yet provided for her!"

My dad's version is much more eloquent than that of Catherine's and brings a tear to my eye.

His explanation continues, but the last lines do confuse me, as they do not seem necessary to the form and seem to me a bit verbose: *"Our <u>first wedding</u> was underwhelming, yet intimate. I would like to be able to provide her a second chance at the wedding of her dreams."*

Although sweet, isn't he laying it on a bit thick? Was he hoping for a sympathy vote? "Ya know, we have never done this before, but he seems like a real stand-up guy. Let's make an exception."

It's doubtful that Tavistock has ever made an exception. And why did Dad underline "first wedding"?

CHAPTER 56

I return home to Leo and Cozette playing outside on this unseasonably mild day. I consider any day in December without gloves and a hat unseasonably mild. "Hi, guys! I came back to pick you up before I go to get some groceries." Which reminds me, I never invited anyone to dinner. I could very well be cooking for three tonight and not seven.

"I'm going to put this envelope inside and text our family group chat, then I'll be right back out."

I head up to my apartment as I text my siblings and Mom. As soon as they reply with an RSVP, I'll run to the store. Until then, it's too nice outside not to play.

"Leo, how about we take Cozette to the park, and on the way home, I can run to the grocery store."

"That sounds fine, as long as I don't have to go in." No surprise there. The grocery store is Leo's least favorite place to go in the world. I'm not exaggerating. He'd rather starve than wait in a grocery store checkout line.

With my siblings not having kids, their nights are often free, apart from Sandra's weekend nights, which are always filled with bachelorette parties, weddings, dates, or girls' weekends. I am happy to hear her tell me that she would be available for dinner.

Joe's wife is going Christmas shopping with her mom, so he is alone and available. I stop short of telling him what I was making for dinner because it doesn't matter much. I could serve him anything edible, and he would come for the free meal that requires him to do nothing. He and Sandra will keep Cozette busy and happy while I make dinner and show Mom what is in the manila envelope.

Is divulging all of this information going too far, I wonder? Dad wouldn't mind, right? I wish I could ask him. But if that were the case, I wouldn't be in this situation.

I think all that he had to say about Mom is lovely. I know I would want to read it if I were Mom, so I will definitely show her, no hesitation.

I look up toward the sky. "I'm sorry I can't get your permission, Dad, but I know Mom will love what you wrote."

The scrumptious spheres of pastry heaven are coming out of the oven as I hear my family walking down the hallway to my apartment. "The door is open; come on in!" I announce as they walk in the door.

"I love your tree!" Sandra exclaims to no one in particular.

"Yes, it looks very nice," my mom announces, agreeing with my sister.

"Take off your coats, and throw them on my bed. I have appetizers out for you to munch on while dinner is cooling."

Joe gets on the floor with Cozette and plays tea party, as I suspected he would. Leo looks relieved to be free of his duty, taking off his tiara.

Leo asks Sandra about teaching, and the stories of the kids begin. She is off this whole upcoming week and could not be more excited about it. Although I am sure she is disappointed that a trip to an island is not booked, at least she can unwind for a week before starting the new year back at school.

It's perfect timing to get Mom alone for a minute or two.

"Hey Mom, I think you will be excited to see what just fell into my lap. Well, it did not exactly *fall;* I had to go get it, but I have it none-theless."

"Well, what is it already?"

I hand her the envelope. She takes out the contents and reads them to herself. "This is incredible! I had no idea Dad was planning this. What an amazing Christmas gift you have just given me!" Mom looks sadder than I expected, a look of remorse on her face and the glisten of a single tear streaming down her cheek.

"Looks like he was trying to find a way to get you the country club wedding you always wanted, but without being a member, he ran into a bump in the road," I say while rubbing Mom's back. I didn't anticipate her crying. I thought this would be such a happy surprise, not a guilt-ridden one.

"The fact that he was willing to do this is so thoughtful. We never really talked about it. He knew that was a far-fetched wish of mine when we got engaged. But with our money situation and your dad about to be deployed, it just wasn't an option."

"Did you not enjoy your wedding?" I ask.

Suddenly, I feel like I do not know my parents at all and remind myself to listen more and talk less.

"It is not that I didn't like it. I just wanted to marry your father; the venue was not the most important thing at the time. The navy was sending Dad to fight in the Iran-Iraq War, and we wanted to be married before the mobilization."

"That sounds convenient."

"Yes, I guess you could say that. He was not gone long, and then we immediately wanted to start a family. My dream wedding was put on the back burner with due reason, of course. But it looks like it was always in the front of Dad's mind, which is very sweet."

"And your reception was in Grandmom's house?"

"Yes, after our small wedding, we went to your grandparents' for lovely butlered appetizers and dinner in the backyard. My dad, your grandpop, made beautiful floral centerpieces for the table."

Interesting. I am going to Grandma's next.

"Do you think Dave will mind me rummaging through the backyard for a bit?"

"It *is* very convenient that your cousin bought the house from your grandparents. And we are family, so of course they won't mind! I can come with you; I would like to see all the renovations they've done. It has been a while since I've visited them. I'm sure the house looks great," Mom adds.

"Wondering if I should also go inside. Not knowing what I am looking for, I suppose it could be inside or out. Assuming Dave's house is even the right place," I say while standing up to begin serving dinner.

"Dinner's ready!"

One of my favorite things about Leo eating over all the time is his willingness to clean up. His nightly quote: "You do all of the delicious cooking; cleaning up is the least I can do."

The only problem with having everyone here for dinner is how late we get to bed. By the time everyone leaves, and we get the kitchen all cleaned up and the food put away, not to mention Cozette tucked in bed, we're exhausted. And it's way later than Leo's normal 8:30 bedtime.

We'll head to Dave's first thing in the morning. It should prove to be interesting. I haven't seen him or his house in an extremely long time. And I don't know why, but something is telling me I am so close to figuring out what Dad wants me to know.

CHAPTER 57

I have not been in this house since we were little, visiting my grandmom and grandpop. Back then, it smelled so strongly of my grandpop's pipe and Lysol. Weird combination, and not one that would normally be pleasing. But the smell of a pipe, even now, makes me smile.

We sit in their driveway, and I am hesitant to go in. I'm not sure why. But I feel like this game is coming to an end soon, and I am not sure if I like that. On another note, I may get some free time back. That is something that I have not had. Holiday seasons are always busy, but this is a whole new level of busy.

Great busy, but busy.

I get out of my car and look at the house, which looks different even from the outside.

"Sweetie, are you okay? You are acting strange, and it's like you're moving in slow motion. I did not want to interrupt you; for a minute I thought you were meditating in the car."

"I'm fine," I lie to my mom.

I never lie, let alone to her, but it is so much simpler than trying to explain what I am feeling when I don't even know myself.

"Okay, let's do this!" I manage to muster up some excitement.

"I texted your aunt to tell her we were coming to see the house and all the renovations, but I did not give any details. I'm hoping she told Dave; I'd hate to startle him."

"It's not like it's 6 a.m., Mom; I don't think we'd startle him. Although he may find it weird that suddenly we are interested in their renovations."

We walk up the driveway of stones, listening to them crunch under our feet.

"I, for one, have been meaning to stop by. I keep making cookies for them and eating them all. Finally, he will get his favorite homemade fudge cookies. Well, not an entire batch, but most of them," Mom confesses. Sounds like it has been weighing on her.

As we walk up the front steps, I help Mom by holding her arm and guiding her up the steps. I feel the need to be extra cautious and attentive since her diagnosis, although I know she doesn't need it. But until I can get to a follow-up appointment with her, I am at a loss for what exactly to do.

We pause to observe what has changed on the porch.

Basically, it is the same, except for the new paint. It looks nice.

"Mom, I did not even think to ask: Is this going to be hard for you? I mean, it is the home you grew up in, and it's likely to be completely different."

"I do not expect it to be hard. The house was old and needed modernization. We had the first dishwasher in town, and last I was here, it had not been replaced. So, I do hope a lot has changed."

I'm glad to hear that. Mom can be very sentimental, but sometimes, like now, she surprises me.

Dave answers the door, and from the look on his face, he is expecting us. So that's good.

"Hey Dave, long time! Love the color of the house!"

"Oh yeah, thanks, we made lots of changes. It took some time, but we're almost up to the twentieth century. Come on in."

We step inside, and the smell does not hit me like it used to.

Gone is the pipe and Lysol smell. Now it has no smell at all. Weird.

Everything has a scent. This is a "no scent" scent, I suppose. Already, the house feels completely different. Funny how the people who visit expect a flood of memories to come back when walking in the door. Meanwhile, if I lived here, I would not want to smell like an old man's pipe either. But damn them for using so much Febreze.

We meander through the house, taking it all in. Mom is reminding me where the house used to end before the addition. I feel like saying, "Yes, I remember, but also, I do not care. I am not here to get into the history of the architecture." Fortunately, though, I do still have a filter, and respond with, "Oh wow! That's crazy!"

It does look nice, and in different circumstances, I'd be asking all kinds of questions about these upgrades. But today, I have more pressing issues.

Today, I want to see what Dad has in store. This home is meaningful in so many ways. So many family meals shared here, so many fun parties hanging out with all our cousins, even annual sleepovers when Mom and Dad would go to Vermont each fall.

But none of those great memories could possibly have anything to do with my dad's game. I just do not see how any of those flashbacks could be a part of this.

"What are your thoughts, Mom?"

"I do not know what to think, Kristy. Are you certain this is where we should be?"

Looking around with a smile, I want to appear as if I am admiring all the upgrades. In reality, I am dissecting every corner of the house, looking for something, anything, to stand out.

"This clue seemed more obvious than any of the others. Maybe I didn't think about it hard enough, but I did not feel the need to. I was certain I had this one right. As soon as we talked about your reception dinner here, I felt that this *had* to be it. I am not giving up. There's lots more house to see."

"I agree. We are not even halfway through; I just don't know if there are any other places that we can try next if we come up short here."

"No, I haven't given it a second thought, Mom. This is it. It has to be."

Many more "oohs" and "ahhs" later, we head out back. "The house looks great. Can we see the backyard?" "Umm, sure, but it's a yard; not much has changed."

Dave replies, looking as confused as I feel.

"Oh, I know, I just have so many fond memories from our Easter egg hunts out there. And those cool basement steps, what were they called?"

"They're called Bilko doors, sweetie." Mom sounds harshly condescending, even though I'm sure she's not trying to.

"We don't use those anymore. We never used them actually. We thought they were just an accident waiting to happen when the kids were little, so we never unlocked them. Plus, when do we ever need to go into the basement, not to mention from the outside?"

"Good point," I agree. "It's just a really cool feature. At least we thought they were cool when we were little. I remember the doors always being wide open. Grandpop never closed them, let alone locked them."

"Good memory, Kristy. Your dad was always afraid you would slam the doors on your fingers if you ever tried to shut them, so he had Grandpop just leave them open with the chains locking them in place whenever we were outside," Mom explains, much less condescending this time.

"But he wasn't afraid of us falling down the steep concrete steps? That's interesting." I'm beginning to question their parenting techniques.

"Kristy, your generation is so soft."

Back to condescending. Ouch, Mom. "Okay, well, I want to go see them."

Dave was not kidding when he said they have never used them. There is ivy growing all across the doors. We could not open these if we tried. I remember the little metal box on the side of the door that held the key.

"I kinda feel like this box to hold the key defeats the whole purpose. What's the point if the box holding the key doesn't have a code to lock it, or something? What's to stop a thief from just getting the key out of the box and letting themselves in?" I seriously inquire.

I'm pretty sure Mom just rolled her eyes at me. "What?" I ask her.

"Grandpop put the key in there so he wouldn't lose it. It was a different time, Kristy. We didn't even think of things like that. It was safe, and people respected others' property."

"Think the key is still in there?" I try opening the box, but it looks like it was covered in rust and then jacked open. I pull at it, and the top of the box just comes off in my hand with very little effort.

"Oh geez, I'm so sorry, Dave! I didn't mean to break it!"

"It doesn't matter. We never even knew that key box was there," he tells us and laughs. "It was covered in ivy long before we moved in."

Mom and Dave walk off to see the new azaleas that he had just planted. I try desperately to pop back into place the piece of metal that I just broke off from the Bilko door key box.

I move closer to try to hook it back on, but cannot get a good look at the latch because of all the overgrown ivy. When I finally get face-level with the box, I see it. This is what I came for. This is why I am here. My dad knows me so well that he knew these basement doors would intrigue me to the point of finding this very well-hidden clue inside of this very hard-to-find key box. There is a piece of paper jammed in the lid, which is probably why it gave way as easily as it did. "Wow, Dad, you're good. And you really have a lot of confidence in me to think I'd be able to find this without any trouble. Maybe too much confidence! "Gosh, I miss you, Dad," I say while looking up to the sky.

"What sweetie? Did you say something?" Mom questions from across the backyard.

"No, Mom, all good!"

Better than good. Amazing.

I am so proud of myself for finding it. This was the most random one to find yet in what seemed like the easiest of all the locations to figure out.

"Hey guys, I'm not feeling so great. Dave, can I get a rain check on the tour of the rest of the house?" I announce to Mom and Dave, just as a reason to excuse myself.

"No problem, let's try not to go so long next time between visits!"

"Oh no, honey, I hope you're okay. Dave, would you mind showing me upstairs? I'll take you up on that cup of coffee, too. And maybe you'd be able to drive me home later?"

"Absolutely! It's not every day that someone comes to see the house and brings fudge cookies. I'll take you home in a bit. Let me go put on a pot of coffee."

"Okay, honey, I'm all set for a ride; you get home and take care of yourself. Call me later and let me know how you're feeling, okay?"

Free at last.

This piece of paper, which sits thick in my hand, folded sixteen times to fit into the small lockbox, has to be read by me and me alone.

CHAPTER 58

"My Dearest Kristy,

Well, you did it. You actually did it! My gosh, you are smarter than you give yourself credit for. This was certainly not easy. Maybe our most challenging game yet! If the roles were reversed, I don't think I'd be as clever as you in figuring this out. I'd still be sitting at the maple tree, wondering what Pic #1 meant!

But I promise you, it was all worth it. Remember how we used to always talk about (well, I did anyway!) how you deserve your own restaurant? And how Joe deserves a big family? And how Sandra should live in a big-girl house?

How would you feel if I told you that it was all possible?

What if I told you a couple of steak dinners weren't all that I won?

I have NEVER been dishonest with you, but I HAVE been extremely cautious in what I've shared.

KRISTIN CORSON-RICCI

For due reasons.

I am not certain that everyone in our lives is completely trustworthy. When people come into money that is randomly won, more often than not, friends expect handouts, and acquaintances act like best friends. Not to mention the phone calls, emails, and visits from people and businesses expecting donations. Privacy, as we know it, would completely vanish. And you know how the Shores love their private family time! So, for the time being, this is between you and me.

As you know, on occasion, I played the lottery on my own, and not always with all my coworkers.
When I did play at random, I always played the month and day of your birthdays.

I won. We won.

And we won big. Like, really big.

I knew those three dates would eventually come through for me; they are my favorite days for many a reason!

Now, I need you to follow some simple instructions.

And from there, I expect you all to do nothing but follow your dreams. And that includes Cozette, of course! Unless her dream is still a dog, then I will leave that to your discretion!

I have taken the money out as a lump sum—more interest for you if you invest wisely.

It has been deposited into a custodial account in Cozette's name. I named you as the successor custodian on the account, so if I am gone (and I'm guessing I am), you will be able to access the account fully.

The money is in the bank where I used to get the coin books for you to fill with dimes and nickels. They will tell you what you need to do to access the money.

I am hoping you will tell Joe immediately so he can start building his family right away. And then Sandra, so she can get her big-girl house, which is no doubt overdue. Of course, I can't forget about your restaurant! And I'm sure Mom is still patiently waiting for her beach house.

If, for some crazy reason, you figured out my clues AFTER the two years following my death, my attorney knows to release the banking information to you two years after my passing. This is when, if I were alive, I would have surprised the family with this unbelievable news.

I have had my concerns about telling your mom only. That's why I wanted to do this as a family... in case you never stumbled upon my letter. Mom's memory and forgetfulness have been rearing their ugly heads more lately. Not knowing how Mom's memory/lack of discretion will be, I have decided to spare her this news alone, which comes with its share of burdens.

My plan was to finally be a member of the Tavistock Country Club, where I would take your mother to dinner for our anniversary.

Instead of the club's restaurant, I would lead her into the ballroom where you all would be, waiting to surprise her. A justice of the peace would be there as well, so we could renew our vows and have the reception she always wanted.

But the surprise was really for all of you, as that is when I planned to tell you about the winning lottery ticket. At that point, enough time would have passed, and hopefully, I would be off the radar of greedy and suspicious outsiders.

But something tells me it will not come to that. And if you're reading this, clearly it hasn't.

Aside from our love of challenges and games, there are a couple of reasons I believe this was the time to reveal my wonderful secret.

You may or may not be aware of my cancer diagnosis. I received the worst news one can get after a recent colonoscopy. Considering how bad my cancer was when it was discovered, and how much it had spread, I knew my time was extremely limited. All I wanted was to live my last months/weeks/days as normally as possible.

To burden my family with this news was the VERY LAST thing I wanted. It would have changed everything, and I wanted to live as normally as possible for as long as possible.

If you did not already know this news, I'm sorry to reveal it in this way. I'm thinking that you, your siblings, and your mom may know the truth about my health by now, since I am assuming I have already passed.

But be assured, no matter how I spent my last days, I am surely comfortable and at peace now.

In addition to my cancer diagnosis motivating me to move forward with my big lottery reveal plan, I also had some other concerns. Concerns that may have been my hormone medication playing tricks on me, or maybe something more.

I feel some coworkers have been looking over my shoulder and are a bit too nosy lately for my liking. Letting the dust from this winning lottery ticket settle before my attorney tells you this amazing news is my only choice. It is best for everyone involved, trust me.

I have done my research on how to best go about this. Lottery winners in the past have told horror story after horror story about the safety of themselves and their families once the news was out. As you know, you all are more important to me than anything in this world, and your safety is my only concern.

What we have as a family is perfect as is. Why mess with perfection? This money will just add to your incredible life and hopefully make things easier for you. That is my wish. Never let this money get in the way of the close bond you all share.

I realize this is a lot to take in. It may even be overwhelming. But once it settles in, and you have control of the account, feel free to tell whom you would like. But keep in mind my advice, and please remember, more money brings more problems.

This is why I chose to stay anonymous. I think that is the smartest idea for you as well.

But getting back to me being gone...

I'm sorry. I am sure it is extremely hard to lose a parent at a young age. I am sure it's impossibly hard for Mom to lose a spouse and best friend. And equally as hard for Cozette to lose the best gramps in the whole wide world (as Cozette so eloquently puts it).

But know that I am in a good place and will be watching over you. As I'm sure I have during your adventure with this game. Do you really think you would have found a key box without my assistance from above? Hehe.

You are an amazing young woman, and your siblings are equally amazing!

I have guided you kids for as long as I was able to on Earth. But my job is now done. You are more than prepared to continue this life without me and my guidance—plus, you will have Mom for a very long time, so you'll be just fine! You got this, sweetie!

Keep raising Cozette with the love and wisdom that you have been, and she will turn out as wonderfully as you are, no doubt!

Before our journey comes to an end, one last thing.
Our winning lotto was for $1.15 billion. With a B. Let that sink in. Not an M, a B.

The lump was over $516 million.

Spend wisely and think of me when you do!

OOO,
Love you forever and ever, Dad

CHAPTER 59

Two Years Later

"Cozette, please put your brother down!"

"C'mon, Mom! I'm big enough to carry Tommy around with me. Daddy lets me!"

"Oh, does he really? I think Daddy and I have to have a little talk when he gets back from the restaurant. For now, just sit with him on the couch, please. Tommy will be walking soon, and then you will be in charge of chasing after him, okay?"

"Fiiine."

"And in six months, when your baby sister is here, I'll really, really need your help with chasing your brother around."

That explanation seems to appease her, which is good because as soon as she sits with her brother on the couch, my phone rings.

"Hello?" I answer, not recognizing the number. But when it does not say *"Possible Spam,"* I answer just in case. Leo always says I am crazy, that he never answers a call from an unknown number.

But what if it's someone in an emergency?

"Hi, is this Kristy Shore?"

"Um, yes, that's my maiden name. Who is this?"

"Hi, this is Detective O'Mally."

"I do not know a Detective O'Mally. Can I help you with something?"

"I'm sorry, ma'am. We met a couple of years ago; I was *Officer* O'Mally then. I have since become a homicide detective. I was in training when we met years ago."

"I do not follow. Is there something I can do for you?" I say, shifting from one foot to the other. Confused, and yet for some reason, my heart is racing.

"I have a recent discovery relating to your father's accident. Are you able to come down to the station so we can talk?"

"A recent discovery in my father's death? My dad was in an awful car accident the night before Thanksgiving years ago. What could we possibly need to talk about?"

"I was assigned to your dad's case when it happened; I was one of the officers to arrive at the scene the night of the accident. I had the unfortunate task of breaking the devastating news to your mother that night.

"There has been a development in your dad's case, and I would like you to come down to the station to discuss it."

"Development? Case? What case? It was kind of cut-and-dry. A tragic accident." Why am I telling this officer, or detective, whatever he is, these things that he should already know?

I am busy cooking for my two babies in the other room, for the third one in my belly, and for my husband, who will be home from the restaurant any minute.

I have no idea what this call could possibly be about, but it is making me extremely uneasy.

"I'm sorry to bother you, ma'am, but I tried calling the phone number that your mother left on the report the night of the accident, and it is disconnected."

Okay, well, I will give him that. I finally convinced Mom to get rid of her landline after I made her count the number of phone calls she got in a week and, of those calls, how many were spam. Day eight, the phone was gone.

Maybe this man really has something he's discovered and needs to tell us. Maybe I should take him seriously and see what exactly is going on.

"Is there anything you can tell me over the phone? I won't be able to come in until the morning. I'd like an idea of what is happening and what was discovered."

"I'm sorry, ma'am, this needs to be done in person."

The Next Morning

"I'm coming with you." Leo doesn't ask me; he tells me.

"How do you propose we do that? I told the detective I'd be there at 8 a.m., the minute he got to work. Mom is meeting me there. And Cozette is not old enough to babysit yet."

Maybe my snark should take a back seat for a minute. He seems concerned. I don't know what he thinks I am about to find out or what he thinks the detective has uncovered, but he seems uneasy.

"Fine. But I'd appreciate it if you would have me on speaker at least. I'd like to be abreast of recent developments, whatever they might be. And you know fifty percent will be lost in translation."

"Absolutely, if they allow it, I will most certainly have you on speaker. But I really do need to head out if I'm going to be there by 8:00. You will make the kids their eggs? And I will pick up bagels from John's before I head home."

I grab the keys to my new Tesla and run out the door.

This monetary gift from Dad has not only been a lifesaver but also a complete game-changer.

Our home is perfect, not massive, but not tiny either. My legs and butt are showing their disdain for not climbing five flights of stairs all day, every day, usually with my hands full of groceries and babies. I think I will take this slight jiggle over the fact that I'm no longer sweating when I unlock my front door.

I cannot help but think of the unfathomable impact this newfound money has had on all our lives.

We can give Cozette, her brother Tommy, and soon-to-be sister Sophie a wonderful home with a huge backyard. And we're lucky enough to be close to St. Rose, so the kids can share in my wonderful grade school experience. But most importantly, Leo can stop stressing about his insurance company and focus more on our restaurant and his volunteer work, which he loves.

Joe and Leah have been blessed with Joey Jr., who is almost six months old already!

And Sandra is continuing to house hunt. She's not ready to leave the city yet, but she is content with upgrading to the swankiest apartment in all of Philadelphia, as indicated by all of her neighbors playing for the 76ers or Eagles.

Mom decided, when given the opportunity to get her dream beach home, that all along she really just wanted a beach vacation home where the whole family could gather.

She is in no way ready to move out of her marital home. I don't blame her. All our memories of Dad are in that house, and I would not want to pack up and leave either if I were her. But she is certainly not slumming by any stretch. The beachfront home in Cape May is one to be envied. Gorgeous views and a spectacular location, but most importantly, enough bedrooms for our entire family. Each kid has their own bedroom, with plenty of extra rooms for our growing family.

After getting every red light, I am finally pulling up to the police station. I park right behind my mom, who is already here, and meet her at the entrance.

I have no idea how much our lives are about to change.

Mom and I walk in and ask to speak to Detective O'Mally. We are told by the woman at the window to follow her into his office.

Why are my palms suddenly sweating?

We sit down in front of a large and intimidating mahogany desk. I am sure the size of the desk is no accident, considering we are in a not-so-warm-and-fuzzy police station.

Detective O'Mally finally makes his appearance with a piping hot Styrofoam cup of coffee. Why are we still making Styrofoam anything? Don't these companies know that this cup is never ever going away? Our poor grandkids will inherit all our awful mistakes.

After he offers us our own coffee-filled Styrofoam cup and we decline, he sits behind his desk.

"I'm sure you're wondering why I have asked you to come down here today."

"Yes, but I'm not sure if *wondering* describes my thoughts exactly. I am very confused," my mom admits. It is the first thing she's said all morning.

She looks completely unnerved and disheveled. I do not know if I've ever seen her like this.

"I completely understand, Mrs. Shore. We were going back into our old files and cold cases from Officer Watson, who has recently retired. I discovered something that was picked up by Officer Watson while we were clearing out her office."

The detective reaches under his desk into a large cabinet and pulls something out.

"This toy was from the scene of the accident and something I was not privy to at the time."

All I can see is cerulean. Electric cerulean.

The original Fudge.

"How can this be? That was my daughter's!"

"That is what we planned to ask you—if you had ever seen this toy before," the detective states as he folds his large hands on the desktop.

My mom looks more confused than ever. "I do not understand. Where did that come from? How do you have it? What is going on?"

"Mrs. Shore, this was found at the scene of the accident. We are not sure why it was in the middle of the road or if it was thrown from the car. But that seems very unlikely, since your husband died inside the vehicle and no windows appeared open at the crash. The windshield was, of course, in pieces, but this dog was found behind the vehicle. I could show you the pictures of the scene, if you would like."

Hard no. I do not want to see pictures from the accident, and I will not allow Mom to see them either. That is most definitely an image that will never leave our minds once we see it.

"No, thank you. We did not want to see the pictures then, and we still choose not to see them." I make it very clear not to take out the pictures from the file.

Now I don't understand. Why was Fudge—which is 100 percent the original Fudge, as I would know that collar anywhere—in the middle of the road?

How long before the accident did it go missing? Was it taken from Cozette? And if so, why?

"I appreciate you coming down to the station today. That is all that I have. Unless you can add anything to our findings, you are free to go. We will update you immediately if anything else is uncovered."

Officer O'Mally stands to dismiss us and leaves us with one final statement: "It is safe to assume that Mr. Shore was avoiding hitting the dog, as it does appear extremely lifelike. And that is likely what led to the accident."

What just happened?

Mom and I exit his office in a fuzzy state. It is one thing to relive Dad's accident, which took over a year for me to erase from my imagination, after the conversation with the officer at the scene. But it is another thing completely to picture my dad trying to avoid what wasn't even a real animal. He saw what he thought was a dog in the road and gave his life for it.

I walk into my house, still bewildered from the morning's events.

Leo greets me at the door, asking why I did not call him and put him on speaker.

"Sweetie, it was not even a conversation. It was a thirty-second one-sided discourse. I am super confused, though. Apparently, the detective, just now, found out that there was debris in the road where Dad crashed."

"Debris? What kind of debris would cause a fatal accident?" he asks, sounding very concerned.

"The original Fudge."

CHAPTER 60

MARTY

Thanksgiving Eve Eve 2024

The home phone rings and rings before finally getting picked up. "Hello?" Tom answers.

"Hey, it's Marty. It's that time of year again when I go through all our office lottery tickets before I throw them away. I need to triple-check that we are not sitting on a big pile of money that we aren't aware of. I noticed one of the drawings this year was a few of the numbers you play when you play on your own."

"Ha, how do you know what numbers I usually play?"

"I don't know; a while back you mentioned you play the kids' birthdays, and that stuck with me."

"Yeah, if I play on my own, I usually *do* play the kids' birthdays. But sadly, I have not played on my own in quite some time."

"Oh, this particular drawing was earlier in the year. Ya holding out on me, Tommy?" I add with an unusually cynical chuckle.

"Wish I could say I was Marty, but my timing has never been great!"

"That is unfortunate. I could have been talking to a millionaire!

Anyway, I'll stop over tomorrow with my famous pecan pie for Thanksgiving. See you then."

"Okay, thanks for calling! See you tomorrow."

Tom turns to his wife. "That was strange. Marty knows the numbers I play when I get lottery tickets on my own and not the ones shared with the office that we all contribute to. How does he even know the kids' birthdays?"

"Wow, that is very observant. But Marty does not have a bad bone in his body. He is just a lonely man who recently lost his wife and must just have a lot of free time on his hands. Is he bringing his pecan pie tomorrow, like he did last year?"

"Yes, he did say he was bringing a pie tomorrow, but no mention of whether he plans to join us for dinner on Thanksgiving."

CHAPTER 61

KRISTY

Thanksgiving Eve, 2:30 p.m.

The doorbell rings and the door opens practically at the same time.

"Hello and happy day before Thanksgiving!" Marty exclaims while walking into the kitchen.

"Oh, hey Marty, come on in. As long as you brought the famous pie," Dad exclaimed excitedly.

"Yes, of course I have it. Made with love, and lots and lots of sugar!"

"Let me get you a glass of wine. What would you like? White or red?" asks Mom, always the most gracious host.

"Oh, no thanks, I'm driving, plus I'm high on life! Raincheck on the wine. Let me put the pie in the fridge and say hello to Cozette."

He takes the pie out of the oversized brown bag in which it was packed. Towels line the bag, as it was hot from the oven when it was packed. The warm pie smells divine.

As Marty leaves the kitchen to see Cozette, I cannot help but notice the terrific mood he is in this afternoon.

"I guess it's just the holiday season approaching, but I can't remember the last time I've seen Marty so genuinely happy," Dad announces to no one in particular.

Marty is off in the living room, playing on the floor with Cozette for most of his visit. When he returns to the kitchen, everyone is busy prepping for the big Thanksgiving meal tomorrow.

"Anything I can do to help before I head out?"

"Oh, I see how it is... drop your pie and run, huh? Haha! Well, I appreciate the offer to help, but I'm heading out in a minute anyway to get potato bread and lotto tickets," Dad declares, as he is rotating the thawing turkey in the sink.

"Okay, well, if I don't make it over tomorrow, have a wonderful Thanksgiving! I'll be heading out before you. I blocked your car in the driveway, so I have no choice."

Marty, bag in hand, kisses everyone goodbye and heads out.

I say goodbye while sitting at the kitchen island with Cozette on my lap, as I fold napkins, happy as can be. Thanksgiving Eve has always been one of my favorite days of the year.

CHAPTER 62

MARTY

I hate being lied to. There is nothing worse, in my opinion, than a lack of honesty. I always wished there could be one universal telltale sign of a lie. Like a red flashing light above your head, the second you stop telling the truth. My biggest pet peeve in life is trying to decipher whether someone is completely honest or fabricating. It is exhausting, really.

I know I am being lied to. I know Tom is lying.

I have spent every week of my career collecting contributions, keeping organized spreadsheets of those who contributed each week, and then giving Tom the ticket money to buy at the store of his choice. The following day, I take time to photocopy the tickets and distribute them to the office participants. It takes time and effort. And all of this for what? So that Tom can go out on his own and buy some tickets for the office and some just for himself? And then our coworkers can't share in the winnings? It just does not seem fair, after all I have done to keep this office dream of winning alive.

He will get his. I will find out one way or another. Tom's perfect life with his perfect wife, perfect family, and perfect Thanksgiving dinner won't last forever.

~

I quickly drive away from the house.

If this is going to happen, it has to happen now.

Let's see how perfect his life is if this miraculously goes according to my far-fetched plan.

Driving in the direction of the supermarket, I zip around the corners, well above the speed limit, adrenaline coursing through my veins.

I reach into the big brown bag stuffed with towels, still warm from hugging the pecan pie on the drive over to the Shores.

I pull out a beloved toy dog that I grabbed from the toy pile while playing on the floor with Cozette. It looks so damn real, it's eerie.

Looking for the perfect drop, both narrow but also with a curvy blind spot.

I see it.

"If all goes according to plan, this could very well be the scene of the crime. Then, maybe, you will regret your choice to lie to me about your big winning ticket. Do you really think I do not know the numbers you play when you go out on your own and buy tickets? Did you really not think I was tracking your numbers more closely than those of the office tickets? You were extremely naive if you didn't. And I hope you now learn the hard way how wrong it is to lie to me.

"I will find that winning ticket, which, according to your lifestyle and consistent attendance at work, has not been cashed in yet.

"Getting my hands on it really will not be that challenging. I have a spare key after all."

I sound like a madman the way I am talking to myself while zipping around curves.

The window is rolled down, and the toy dog is thrown into the road, where it could potentially have the perfect impact of a swerve, followed by a concrete barrier.

Now all I must do is wait.

EPILOGUE

"Mail call in five. All inmates will remain in their designated zones. Names will be read. No name, no mail. Any disruption will be dealt with accordingly," a flat, cold voice announces over the intercom. The speaker goes dead with a pop, leaving a hum of tension in its place.

Five minutes. Five minutes sitting on this worn bench, leaning against the chipping concrete wall, eyes fixated on the officer shuffling through the stack of envelopes. He is acting as if this isn't the biggest highlight of our week. I sit on the edge of my seat, elbows resting on my knees, hands laced tightly, as if squeezing them might coax my name out of the guard's mouth.

I don't want to be forgotten. Maybe this will be my day, after weeks and weeks of no letters. My heart beats fast and heavy with each name called. Each envelope handed to a fellow prisoner, and not to me, brings a sting to my chest.

"Jerome... Jamal... Hector... Martin..."

For a split second, I thought I had imagined it. I blink slowly as if clearing my head. The guard calls out again, louder this time, "Martin!"

I stand slowly, my legs suddenly unsteady, as I walk to take the envelope.

I don't look at anyone else as I walk back to my spot on the bench, just staring at the envelope with my name in blue inked cursive writing. My eyes lock on the envelope for a long minute before opening it. The stationery smells fresh, like laundry detergent and something else. Something familiar and warm. Home, maybe.

I slide my finger under the adhesive and pull out what may very well be the last piece of correspondence I will ever receive from outside of these prison walls...

"Dear Marty,

I told myself I wouldn't write. I told myself to move on and continue to try to gain some semblance of forgiveness from my three beautiful children. But here I am, putting pen to paper because the truth is, you don't get to disappear behind those walls and act like I am supposed to sit quietly on the outside, pretending like I wasn't a pawn in your horrific game.

We brought you into our home as if you were family. And all along, you were controlling me as a marionette in your horrendous plan. Making me play a role in your horrifying scheme. I will never, ever forgive myself for succumbing to your advances and ruining all that I had. That will haunt me until the day that I die. I will own that disgraceful piece of my life with regret forever. But you, Marty, will die in prison because of it.

Please stop writing your letters of apology to me and my children.

We are trying our best to move on. Move on without a father and husband. Move on from the nightmare you have caused.

I will spend the rest of my life atoning for my mistakes and seeking forgiveness.

You, Marty, will die behind those bars that imprison you and then burn in hell for eternity, for all the grief and heartache that you have caused.

-Helen"

THANK YOU FOR READING MY BOOK!

Thank you for buying and reading my book!
Scan the QR code to connect:

I appreciate your interest in my book and value your feedback, as it helps me improve future versions. I would appreciate it if you could leave your invaluable review on Amazon.com with your feedback.
Thank you!